US MILITARY CAREERS

US COAST GUARD

BY DONNA B. McKINNEY

CONTENT CONSULTANT

Lt. Kimberly Young-McLear
Assistant Professor
US Coast Guard Academy

Essential Library

An Imprint of Abdo Publishing | abdobooks.com

ABDOBOOKS.COM

Published by Abdo Publishing, a division of ABDO, PO Box 398166, Minneapolis, Minnesota 55439. Copyright © 2021 by Abdo Consulting Group, Inc. International copyrights reserved in all countries. No part of this book may be reproduced in any form without written permission from the publisher. Essential Library™ is a trademark and logo of Abdo Publishing.

Printed in the United States of America, North Mankato, Minnesota.
032020
092020

Cover Photo: Petty Officer 3rd Class John Hightower/US Coast Guard/Defense Visual Information Distribution Service
Interior Photos: Senior Airman Sean Sweeney/US Air Force/Defense Visual Information Distribution Service, 4–5; Petty Officer 1st Class Bradley Pigage/US Coast Guard/Defense Visual Information Distribution Service, 8; Petty Officer 2nd Class Annie R. B. Elis/US Coast Guard/Defense Visual Information Distribution Service, 11; Marianne Campolongo/Shutterstock Images, 12–13; AP Images, 17; US Coast Guard/Defense Visual Information Distribution Service, 21, 92–93; Susan Walsh/AP Images, 22; Petty Officer 1st Class Patrick Kelley/US Coast Guard/Defense Visual Information Distribution Service, 24–25; Senior Chief Petty Officer NyxoLyno Cangemi/US Coast Guard, 28; T.Whitney/Shutterstock Images, 31; Petty Officer 2nd Class Lisa Ferdinando/US Coast Guard/Defense Visual Information Distribution Service, 33; Petty Officer 2nd Class Richard Brahm/US Coast Guard/Defense Visual Information Distribution Service, 36; Petty Officer 1st Class Alexis Lopez/US Coast Guard/Defense Visual Information Distribution Service, 38–39; Petty Officer 3rd Class Michael Anderson/US Coast Guard/Defense Visual Information Distribution Service, 43, 56; Petty Officer 2nd Class Ali Flockerzi/US Coast Guard/Defense Visual Information Distribution Service, 46–47; Petty Officer 3rd Class Amanda Norcross/US Coast Guard/Defense Visual Information Distribution Service, 49; Petty Officer 3rd Class Sarah Wilson/US Coast Guard/Defense Visual Information Distribution Service, 52; Petty Officer 2nd Class Paul Dragin/US Coast Guard/Defense Visual Information Distribution Service, 54–55; Mass Communication Specialist 2nd Class Ruben Reed/US Navy/Defense Visual Information Distribution Service, 59; Chief Petty Officer Sara Muir/US Coast Guard/Defense Visual Information Distribution Service, 64–65; Chief Petty Officer John Masson/US Coast Guard/Defense Visual Information Distribution Service, 68; Petty Officer 1st Class Michael De Nyse/US Coast Guard/Defense Visual Information Distribution Service, 70; Chief Petty Officer Mindy Tucker/US Coast Guard/Defense Visual Information Distribution Service, 74–75; Brent Erb/US Coast Guard/Defense Visual Information Distribution Service, 78; Petty Officer 3rd Class Ross Ruddell/US Coast Guard/Defense Visual Information Distribution Service, 82–83; Petty Officer 1st Class Brandyn Hill/US Coast Guard/Defense Visual Information Distribution Service, 86; Seaman Brendan Stainfield/US Coast Guard/Defense Visual Information Distribution Service, 89; Petty Officer 3rd Class Nathan W. Bradshaw/US Coast Guard/Defense Visual Information Distribution Service, 97

Editor: Charly Haley
Series Designer: Nikki Nordby

LIBRARY OF CONGRESS CONTROL NUMBER: 2019954352

PUBLISHER'S CATALOGING-IN-PUBLICATION DATA

Names: McKinney, Donna B., author.
Title: US Coast Guard / by Donna B. McKinney
Description: Minneapolis, Minnesota : Abdo Publishing, 2021 | Series: US military careers | Includes online resources and index.
Identifiers: ISBN 9781532192289 (lib. bdg.) | ISBN 9781098210182 (ebook)
Subjects: LCSH: Coast guard--Juvenile literature. | Members of the Armed Forces--Juvenile literature. | Military power--Juvenile literature. | Coast surveillance--Juvenile literature.
Classification: DDC 355.12--dc23

CONTENTS

CHAPTER ONE
Flying into the Storm 4

CHAPTER TWO
The History of the US Coast Guard 12

CHAPTER THREE
The US Coast Guard Today 24

CHAPTER FOUR
Boatswain's Mate 38

CHAPTER FIVE
Maritime Enforcement Specialist 46

CHAPTER SIX
Damage Controlman 54

CHAPTER SEVEN
Aviator 64

CHAPTER EIGHT
Pharmacist 74

CHAPTER NINE
Aviation Survival Technician 82

CHAPTER TEN
Marine Science Technician 92

Essential Facts	100	Source Notes	106
Glossary	102	Index	110
Additional Resources	104	About the Author	112

CHAPTER 1

FLYING INTO THE STORM

A US Coast Guard helicopter pilot was halfway through his 24-hour shift when the call for help came in. Within minutes, a crew had the helicopter in the air. A man was stranded in his boat, dangerously near a steep cliff along the shoreline. The winds were swirling at 40 knots, which is about

A helicopter lowers a coast guard rescue swimmer into the water.

46 miles per hour (74 kmh). At 6:30 p.m., darkness was falling fast, making the rescue even more challenging.

Before that alarm sounded, the pilot had spent the quieter minutes of the day carefully studying the weather conditions and navigation reports. Coast guard pilots do this so that when calls for help come in, they are prepared and ready to fly within moments. While the pilot studied the reports, crew members worked on the helicopter. They performed careful safety checks, making sure everything was in the right condition for flying.

5

As the helicopter cut through the fading daylight, the cliffs came into view. The crew could not see the stranded boater. The pilot flew over the area where the crew believed the boater was. The helicopter crew scanned the water looking for him. After three passes overhead, the rescuers finally spotted the frightened boater and saw that he had his dog with him. The rescue now included both a person and a dog.

With calm precision, the pilot positioned the helicopter, hovering near the boater. The crew lowered a coast guard rescue swimmer into the churning water. While the pilot held the powerful aircraft in position, the rescue swimmer secured the

A DAY WITH THE COAST GUARD

An average day with the US Coast Guard is busy. On an average day:

- Coast guard small boats are on 396 missions.
- Coast guard aircraft—planes and helicopters—fly 164 missions, logging 324 hours of flight time.
- Coast guard men and women board 100 ships in ports and inspect the ships to be sure they are following safety laws and regulations.
- Coast guard men and women respond to 20 spills involving oil or hazardous chemicals.
- Coast guard men and women help guide 2,509 ships heading in or out of US ports.
- When the Great Lakes are covered in ice in the winter, coast guard icebreaker ships clear ice away from the routes for all ships.[1]

boater and his dog into a rescue basket. The helicopter crew raised the rescue basket and pulled the boater and his dog into the safety of the helicopter. Then the crew dropped a rescue hook and hoisted the rescue swimmer back to the helicopter. The pilot turned the helicopter toward shore. The coast guard crew had saved another life.

When storms whip up bad weather, most people head indoors to safety. But US Coast Guard search-and-rescue helicopter pilots do just the opposite. They head out into storms to rescue people who are in danger.

A CALL TO JOIN

Lieutenant Commander Tom Huntley, a coast guard helicopter pilot, was stationed in Kodiak, Alaska, where he flew in extreme weather conditions to rescue people in deadly situations. Huntley joined the coast guard after the terrorist attacks of September 11, 2001, in which terrorists crashed two airplanes into the World Trade Center towers in New York City, killing nearly 3,000 people. "[The 9/11 attacks] shook me in two ways," Huntley said in 2016. "One was a draw to patriotism. But probably more so was a call to do something that actually mattered. In my job at the time, I felt like I could either go to work or not go to work and nothing really mattered."[2] He decided to shift careers and enter the coast guard. Huntley said, "The coast guard really did appeal

★ A helicopter crew prepares for a search-and-rescue training mission at a coast guard air station in Kodiak, Alaska.

to me, partially because it entailed being part of the military combined with the humanitarian and lifesaving mission."[3]

Huntley knows his job can be a dangerous one. "Alaska does mean something special, especially in a search-and-rescue helicopter," he said. "This is the most extreme area to conduct these sort of operations, and not just because of the weather—although the weather plays a major role. The seas are bigger, and the nights are way longer. In the winter in Kodiak, we routinely have winds at 70, 80, 90 knots, which is hurricane-force. And we go fly in it, because we have to."[4]

JOBS IN THE COAST GUARD

Piloting a search-and-rescue helicopter is just one of many jobs available to people who join the US Coast Guard. The coast guard is one of six US military services. The other five are the US Army, the US Navy, the US Marine Corps, the US Air Force, and the US Space Force. The coast guard is tasked with keeping US ports and waterways safe and secure. It is unique among the military services because it is part of the US Department of Homeland Security. All other military branches belong to the US Department of Defense. The coast guard is

WHAT DOES IT TAKE TO JOIN THE COAST GUARD?

The coast guard has some basic requirements for people who want to join. Here are the requirements for joining the enlisted ranks:

- Be a US citizen or a lawful permanent resident
- Be between 17 and 31 (people age 17 need a parent's permission)
- Have a high school diploma
- Have no more than three children or other dependents
- Pass the military entrance medical exam

A person who meets these basic requirements must also take and pass a test called the Armed Service Vocational Aptitude Battery (ASVAB). The coast guard runs a criminal background check on people who want to join (and a felony conviction disqualifies a person from serving in the coast guard). The coast guard also considers a person's "attitude, professionalism, honesty, respect, language proficiency, height/weight, physical abilities, and work ethic."[5]

OFFICER VS. ENLISTED

A person can enter the coast guard as an enlisted person or as an officer. Being enlisted does not require a college degree, but an enlisted person must have a high school diploma. Enlisted personnel receive training to perform specific jobs.

Officers manage and lead the enlisted personnel. They plan missions and assign tasks. Being an officer requires a four-year college degree. Officers also must complete training through the coast guard's Officer Candidate School.

Both officers and enlisted personnel can work toward promotions. Enlisted personnel who want to become officers should work toward getting a four-year college degree and apply for Officer Candidate School.

part of Homeland Security because, unlike the other military branches, most of its work is in the United States, protecting the country's coasts, ports, and waterways. The coast guard has about 41,000 active duty members.[6]

The coast guard's motto is the Latin phrase *Semper Paratus*. It means "always ready," an apt description for the jobs that the coast guard does. A person can enter the coast guard as an enlisted person or as an officer. Young men and women entering the coast guard's enlisted ranks have 20 different jobs (called "ratings") to choose from. These jobs include a wide range of duties, from tracking down drug traffickers to preventing water pollution to saving people's lives.

People who enter the coast guard's enlisted ranks are sent to eight weeks of basic training. After that training, the new coastguardsmen are promoted to

★ Coast guard members have a wide variety of jobs working at sea and on land, on boats and on aircraft.

entry-level positions such as seaman apprentice (working on the deck of a ship) or fireman apprentice (working to maintain a ship's engine and mechanics). Upon being promoted, they are sent to their first assignments, where they learn more about the various career paths available to them. The next step is to attend apprentice-level "A" school in their specific rating.

Young people who join the coast guard after completing college have the opportunity to enter as officers. Usually this path begins with the 17-week Officer Candidate School in New London, Connecticut. Upon completion of Officer Candidate School, the new coast guard officers are assigned to a ship, a staff job, or an onshore assignment, or they go on to attend flight training. No matter which job they choose, coastguardsmen are serving their country as part of a long-standing US military tradition.

CHAPTER 2

THE HISTORY OF THE US COAST GUARD

The US Coast Guard traces its roots all the way back to 1789, when George Washington was the president of the United States. The US Congress created the Lighthouse Establishment and gave it control over the 12 lighthouses that were in the United States at that time.[1] Before the Lighthouse

The US Coast Guard still manages lighthouses today, including the Sankaty Head Lighthouse in Nantucket, Massachusetts.

Establishment was created, the American colonies and then the states had built and managed the lighthouses. This Lighthouse Establishment was funded by the US Treasury, part of the newly formed US government.

A year later, on August 4, 1790, the US Congress approved Secretary of the Treasury Alexander Hamilton's proposal to build ten boats called cutters. These cutters would be part of a military service that would patrol the new country's coastal waters. Around this time, pirates cruised the coast of North America,

13

SHIPS CALLED CUTTERS

In the coast guard, a cutter is a vessel that is more than 65 feet (20 m) long. A ship that is less than 65 feet long is simply called a boat. In earlier times, cutters were rigged with larger sails than other vessels, allowing them to move faster. They got the name *cutter* because they could "cut" through the water faster than other ships. Because one of the coast guard's duties is to catch people smuggling illegal items into the United States, fast ships are important. Even after the sailing ships were replaced with steam engines, the name *cutter* stuck. Today's coast guard cutters range in length from 65 feet (20 m) long to 420 feet (128 m) long.[2] Cutters have space for the crew to live on the ship. Cutters help the coast guard perform a wide range of tasks, from law enforcement to search-and-rescue work to construction. The coast guard's boats usually operate near shore or on inland waters. Sometimes they work alongside cutters.

attacking ships and stealing the goods they carried. The main job of the cutters was to ensure that goods shipped from the United States to other countries were protected from pirates and arrived at their destinations safely.

These cutters came to be officially called the Revenue Cutter Service, a part of the Treasury Department, years later, in 1863. But the coast guard marks August 4, 1790, as its official birthday. This birthday puts the coast guard among the oldest organizations that are still part of the federal government.

EXPANDING THE COAST GUARD

By 1840, the country's system of lighthouses had grown from those initial 12 lighthouses to 234 lighthouses, all warning ships of danger along the US coastline. There were also 30 lightships used near places where it was difficult to build a lighthouse. These ships were positioned along the coast with lights at the top of their masts and a whistle or horn that sounded to warn of danger.[3]

The leader of the coast guard carries the title of commandant. The very first coast guard commandant was Captain-Commandant Alexander Fraser. He was appointed

IDA LEWIS: LIGHTHOUSE KEEPER

Lighthouses along the US shores used to be staffed by lighthouse keepers in the days before lighthouses were automated. These keepers ensured that lights were shining to warn boaters of dangers near the shoreline. They also rescued people from the waters. Ida Lewis, born in 1842, started helping her parents run the Lime Rock Lighthouse in Rhode Island when she was just 15 years old. One of her jobs was to row her siblings from the lighthouse back to the mainland school every weekday. In 1879, after both of her parents had died, Lewis took over as lighthouse keeper. She was already known for her swimming, rowing, and boat handling skills. She worked at Lime Rock for 54 years, until her death in 1911. Over the years, she is credited with saving at least 18 lives. Her last lifesaving rescue was when she was 63 years old.[4]

commandant of the Revenue Cutter Service in 1843. People considered him to be a visionary who was ahead of his time.

During his command, Fraser updated the coast guard fleet to ships with iron hulls and steam engines, stopped the use of enslaved workers aboard the ships, and improved pay and working conditions for enlisted people. He also started the first coast guard officers' training program.

On January 28, 1915, US president Woodrow Wilson signed the Act to Create the Coast Guard. This law formally combined the Life-Saving Service and the Revenue Cutter Service, making them into the US Coast Guard. When President Wilson signed this law, the coast guard officially became part of the US military. Over decades of time, the US

AFRICAN AMERICANS IN THE COAST GUARD

Before slavery was abolished in the United States in 1865, enslaved African American people were used in early versions of coast guard operations. After 1865, the coast guard began hiring African American workers, though they were mostly segregated from white workers. In 1875, African Americans were hired to work at lifesaving stations. These workers, who were fishermen and oystermen, manned the stations along the Maryland, Virginia, and North Carolina coasts. They responded to ships in distress, saving many lives. Captain Richard Etheridge assumed command of the Pea Island Life-Saving Station in North Carolina in 1880. From that date until 1947, when the station was closed, it was staffed by an all–African American crew. The coast guard began racial integration of its crews in 1942.

★ Coastguardsmen stand on a speedboat packed with nearly 700 cases of illegal liquor in 1932. The coast guard seized many similar boats during Prohibition.

government brought two more agencies into the coast guard, the Lighthouse Service (added in 1939) and the Bureau of Marine Inspection and Navigation (added in 1946).

As time passed, the problem of pirates eased, but then came the era of Prohibition, during which the production and sale of alcohol was outlawed in the United States. The US government signed Prohibition into law in January 1920. To combat the growing problem of liquor smuggling, the coast guard grew.

During the Prohibition years, from 1920 to 1933, the coast guard seized thousands of boats, called rum runners, that were transporting illegal alcohol. The coast guard expanded in numbers and capability during Prohibition. It had about 330 vessels measuring 75 feet (23 m) or longer during this time, protecting the US coastline.[5] In addition to battling the rum runners, the coast guard was still busy carrying out its other missions to protect the country's waterways.

WORLD WAR II

In June 1944, coast guard cutters, manned warships, and landing craft (which moved people and equipment from ships to shore) took part in the assault against German forces on the beaches at Normandy, France, during World War II (1939–1945). In this war, the Allied forces of Great Britain, the United States, the Soviet Union, and France fought against the Axis forces of Germany, Italy, and Japan. Coastguardsmen and boats played a significant role in the success of the Allied forces. The battle at Normandy was a turning point toward victory for the Allies.

Throughout World War II, the coast guard carried out the important duty of getting soldiers to the beaches and then providing support for the battles there. The coastguardsmen excelled at handling small boats because of their work using those same boats at the lifesaving stations back in the United States. In wartime, the coastguardsmen's ability to navigate the smaller boats carrying troops through strong ocean currents and around reefs and sandbars was essential to the success of the American troops.

THE WAR ON DRUGS

In the 1970s, drug smugglers' use of boats increased rapidly, following an increase in recreational drug use in the United States in the 1960s. In 1971, President Richard Nixon called drug abuse "public enemy number one" and officially declared a national "War on Drugs."[6] The president increased funding for the government agencies tasked with battling drug abuse.

The coast guard's role in fighting drug smuggling became increasingly important. In 1984, the cutter *Clover* captured

THE COAST GUARD'S FIRST DRUG RAID

Drug interdiction—stopping smugglers from bringing illegal drugs into the United States—is one of the coast guard's missions. The coast guard has been working to stop illegal drugs for more than a century. August 31, 1890, marks the first record of a revenue cutter seizing a shipment of narcotics. Officers from the revenue cutter *Wolcott* boarded the steamer *George E. Starr* and discovered it was carrying opium, an illegal drug. The revenue cutter crew seized the steamer and its illegal cargo.

13 tons (12 metric tons) of marijuana.[7] Just a few days later, the cutter *Northwind* became the first icebreaker to capture drug smugglers when its crew seized 20 tons (18 metric tons) of marijuana.[8] In 1989, the government tasked the coast guard with leading the country's efforts to prevent drug smuggling by sea. Today the coast guard fights drugs with the latest technology and vessels such as the coast guard cutter *Munro*. In 2019, the *Munro* captured a custom-made submarine used for drug smuggling. With the capture of the submarine, the *Munro*'s crew seized 17,000 pounds (7,710 kg) of cocaine.[9]

ORGANIZATIONAL CHANGES

A major shift in the coast guard's organization came in 1967 when the US government moved the coast guard from the Department of the Treasury to the Department of Transportation. As the coast guard's activities had expanded beyond supporting the Treasury Department, government officials thought the Department of Transportation would be a better fit.

The next big shift came in 2003, when the coast guard was moved to the Department of Homeland Security. The Department of Homeland Security was created after the terrorist attacks of September 11, 2001. After those attacks, the United States increased its security measures in many different areas, including US ports, to guard against possible future attacks

★ Coast guard members unload 2,500 pounds (1,130 kg) of marijuana that they seized during a drug bust on the Atlantic Ocean, near the coast of Florida.

★ President George W. Bush, *left*, who created the Department of Homeland Security, salutes coast guard members in 2005.

from terrorists. The coast guard's focus on protecting US ports became even more important.

While the coast guard is not officially part of the Department of Defense, during times of war or conflict, the president of the United States can transfer the coast guard to the Department of the Navy, which is under the Department of Defense. This allows the coast guard to more easily serve in cooperation with other military branches. This has happened frequently in the past when the United States was engaged in conflicts.

CHAPTER 3

THE US COAST GUARD TODAY

The US Coast Guard is the main federal government agency responsible for "maritime safety, security, and environmental stewardship in US ports and waterways," according to its website.[1] The coast guard protects and defends more than 100,000 miles (161,000 km) of US coastline and

A coast guard cutter off the coast of San Pedro, California

inland waterways, such as rivers and canals.[2] The coast guard also rescues people in danger and protects the environment.

MILITARY AND CIVILIAN ROLES

With its unique position as a branch of the military and a part of the Department of Homeland Security, the US Coast Guard has both civilian and military responsibilities. The coast guard is a first responder to people affected by natural or man-made disasters, whether on land or at sea. As a federal law enforcement agency, the coast guard works to stop any illegal activity happening at the country's ports and coastlines. The coast guard also protects the environment by ensuring that people and companies follow regulations against dumping trash or hazardous materials into the country's waterways. During wartime, the coast guard serves under the Department of the Navy, fulfilling military roles to protect the country against terrorism and other threats.

The coast guard is organized into two main geographic areas—Atlantic and Pacific. Within these two geographic areas, there are nine coast guard districts. Within those nine districts, the coast guard is organized into 37 sectors that are located at ports in the United States. Coast guard headquarters are located on the Department of Homeland Security's Saint Elizabeth's campus in Washington, DC. At the headquarters, coast guard officers and civilian employees manage programs, develop policy, and handle personnel matters.

MISSIONS

The coast guard has 11 official missions organized into two broad categories: homeland security missions and non–homeland security missions. Homeland security refers to the coast guard's work in keeping the United States safe from outside threats, such as foreign terrorist attacks. The rest of the coast guard's duties—such as rescuing stranded boaters and helping ships safely navigate along the US coasts—are considered non–homeland security.

The homeland security missions include port and waterway security, drug interdiction, migrant interdiction, defense readiness, and other law enforcement duties. Providing security for US ports and waterways involves preventing terrorist attacks in these areas and responding if an attack occurs. Drug interdiction is the coast guard's work defending against smugglers who try to bring illegal drugs into the United States. Migrant interdiction is the coast guard's work to prevent people from entering the United States illegally.

The non–homeland security missions include aids to navigation, search and rescue,

COAST GUARD ACADEMY

Some coastguardsmen enter the military through the US Coast Guard Academy, located in New London, Connecticut. The academy is a competitive, four-year military college that offers bachelor of science degrees in these majors: civil engineering, electrical engineering, cyber systems, mechanical engineering, naval architecture and marine engineering, operations research and computer analysis, marine and environmental sciences, management, and government. When they graduate from the academy, cadets are commissioned as ensigns, the lowest rank of officer. About 200 cadets graduate from the academy each year.[3] Cadets' tuition, room, and board are fully paid for by the government. Cadets commit to serve five years as officers in the coast guard following graduation from the academy.

★ Coast guard members exit an icebreaker ship in the Arctic to survey the surrounding ice and make sure it is safe for scientists and researchers aboard the ship.

living marine resources, marine safety, marine environmental protection, and ice operations. Aids to navigation are the coast guard's signs, buoys, lighthouses, and regulations that aim to safely guide all boaters on US waterways. The coast guard's search-and-rescue mission is carried out by helping boaters who are in distress and need rescue. The coast guard's living marine resources mission involves guarding against illegal fishing in US waterways. With its marine safety mission, the coast guard promotes safe boating practices. The coast guard's marine environmental protection mission includes protecting the marine environment, including both the species that live there and the waters themselves. The coast guard's ice operations take place in frozen waters, such as the Great Lakes during winter, where icebreaker ships are needed to keep the channels clear of ice so that other ships can safely travel.

COAST GUARD ACTIVE DUTY

As of 2019, approximately 41,000 people were serving in the active duty US Coast Guard.[4] Active duty is like working a full-time job. Recruits enter active duty service as either enlisted personnel or officers. Men and women coming into the coast guard as active duty enlisted members earn a salary of approximately $20,000 a year. Coast guard officers start out with a salary of approximately $38,000 a year.[5]

Other allowances are added to raise the basic pay amounts. For example, government housing is provided for coast guard personnel, or they receive a housing allowance. There could be a hazardous duty allowance for coastguardsmen who perform more dangerous jobs such as flying, handling toxic fuels, or working on the flight deck of a ship. There are clothing allowances that help coastguardsmen pay for the costs of their uniforms. There is also a sea pay allowance for coastguardsmen permanently assigned to ships. In addition to their salary, coastguardsmen also receive free health, vision, dental, and life insurance. They earn 30 days of paid vacation, receive help to pay for college tuition, and gain opportunities to travel. Most coast guard jobs are based in the United States and the US territory of Puerto Rico, but some coastguardsmen work in other parts of the world.

COAST GUARD RESERVE

The US Coast Guard Reserve allows people to serve in the coast guard on a part-time basis. Reservists can serve as enlisted personnel or officers. Like people entering the active duty coast guard, reservists take the Armed Services Vocational Aptitude Battery (ASVAB) test and then undergo basic training at Cape May, New Jersey.

Reservists typically perform coast guard duties at a base near their home one weekend a month and two weeks during the year. The US Coast Guard has bases around the country. Some reservists work in coast guard jobs that are similar to their civilian jobs. Other reservists learn new skills, and their coast guard reserve jobs are very different from their civilian jobs. Reservists serve alongside full-time coastguardsmen, earning a salary and benefits. These benefits can include assistance in paying for college or technical training. Reservists can be called to active duty if needed. This could happen during a war or national emergency. About 7,000 people serve in the coast guard reserve.[6]

Petty Officer Third Class Adrien Cheval is a coast guard reservist who is assigned to a small boat station. In this role,

US COAST GUARD RANKS

ENLISTED PERSONNEL
Seaman Recruit
Seaman Apprentice
Seaman
Petty Officer Third Class
Petty Officer Second Class
Petty Officer First Class
Chief Petty Officer
Senior Chief Petty Officer
Master Chief Petty Officer
Command Master Chief Petty Officer
Master Chief Petty Officer of the Coast Guard

WARRANT OFFICERS
Chief Warrant Officer 2
Chief Warrant Officer 3
Chief Warrant Officer 4

COMMISSIONED OFFICERS
Ensign
Lieutenant Junior Grade
Lieutenant
Lieutenant Commander
Commander
Captain
Rear Admiral Lower Half
Rear Admiral
Vice Admiral
Admiral
Fleet Admiral

he primarily supports two missions—search and rescue and maritime law enforcement. "The coast guard is unique," Cheval said, "in that the reservists actually work hand-in-hand with the active duty counterparts, so we actually get to do the same mission. . . . It's pretty nice because I can come in and drill two days a month and do this mission and then go home and do my civilian job during the week. So, it's a really nice balance. . . . The fact that I'm getting paid to drive a boat and save lives and to also enforce federal law is a great privilege."[7]

THE ASVAB TEST

Anyone joining the coast guard must pass the Armed Services Vocational Aptitude Battery (ASVAB) test. All branches of the US military use the ASVAB as an entrance exam for recruits. The ASVAB is a series of subtests focused on areas such as general science, mathematics knowledge, word knowledge, automotive and shop information, and mechanical comprehension. Practice copies of the ASVAB are available online so recruits can become familiar with the exam before taking it. David Davis, chief of the testing division at US Military Entrance Processing Command, explained the ASVAB this way: "The test itself measures how well [students] have obtained the information that they have been taught in school already. So math, science, reading comprehension, arithmetic reasoning, all those subjects are being taught in school so we measure where they are."[8]

★ While on duty, coast guard reservists do many of the same jobs as active duty coastguardsmen.

COAST GUARD AUXILIARY

The US Coast Guard Auxiliary is a volunteer civilian group that works to support the coast guard. Congress established the auxiliary in 1939. It has units in all 50 states plus the US territories of Puerto Rico, the Virgin Islands, American Samoa, and Guam. During World War II, the auxiliary's 50,000 members used their private boats to help the coast guard protect the US coasts.[9]

Today, the auxiliary works to promote boating safety and support the coast guard in keeping the ports, waterways, and coasts safe. Auxiliary volunteers take part in search and rescue, safety and security patrols, safety exams for commercial fishing vessels, homeland security, and pollution response to help with cleanup when a hazardous material is spilled into a waterway. About 31,000 people work in the coast guard auxiliary's

33

volunteer force.[10] Men and women age 17 and older can join the coast guard auxiliary. People wanting to join cannot have been convicted of a felony, and they must be physically and mentally able to do the job they choose within the auxiliary.

CAREER CHOICES

With the coast guard's wide-ranging mission of law enforcement, environmental protection, and military functions, men and women entering the coast guard have a variety of jobs to choose from. The coast guard provides the training needed for these

PAYING FOR COLLEGE

The College Student Pre-Commissioning Initiative (CSPI) scholarship program is designed to help high school students who are headed to college and who want to become coast guard officers. CSPI is open to students attending colleges and universities that are officially designated as minority serving institutions (MSI). These are schools that serve a certain percentage of people of color or that developed in racial minority communities. CSPI pays for college tuition up to two years, books and fees, housing, and medical benefits, along with paying the student a salary.

During the school year, students in the CSPI program participate in coast guard activities for at least 16 hours a month. During school breaks, the students train and work at a coast guard station. When CSPI students finish their junior year of college, they attend a three-week leadership course. After college graduation, CSPI students attend the 17-week Officer Candidate School. Then they are commissioned as ensigns (the lowest officer rank) in the coast guard.

RESPONDING TO HURRICANE KATRINA

When Hurricane Katrina stormed ashore in August 2005, it inflicted catastrophic damage along the US Gulf Coast. The storm surge, up to 27 feet (8.2 m) above sea level, broke records. Through training and drills, the coast guard stays ready for disasters like Hurricane Katrina. As the huge storm swept ashore, the coast guard began the largest search-and-rescue mission in US history. Coast guard airplanes flew missions to determine the damage. Coast guard helicopters found and rescued survivors. Coast guard boats worked to rescue survivors and transport much-needed supplies. The coast guard sent 5,600 personnel to help the Gulf Coast region recover from the storm. President George W. Bush awarded the US Coast Guard the Presidential Unit Citation—the highest honor given to a military unit—describing the coast guard's response as "one of the finest hours in the coast guard's 216-year history."[11] In more recent years, the coast guard has provided support during other catastrophic storms, such as Hurricane Harvey and Hurricane Florence.

jobs. The coast guard offers career opportunities in many fields, including law, aviation, engineering, communications, computer and information technologies, intelligence, and health care.

Some jobs in the coast guard are very specialized in relation to the coast guard's role as a branch of the US military. But there are many other coast guard members—such as lawyers, engineers, computer specialists, doctors, and dentists—who fill jobs similar to those outside of the military. People can work in many different career fields while serving their country as members of the coast guard.

WELCOME TO BASIC

TRAINING AT CAPE MAY

For young men and women who want to serve in the coast guard, the first hurdle is basic training, also known as boot camp. The training is called "basic," but it is not easy. Recruits arrive at Cape May, New Jersey, for eight weeks of intense training with both physical and academic challenges. Recruits are paid during basic training.

As part of the arrival process, recruits undergo medical exams. Men get haircuts. Women are allowed to pin up their hair so it meets coast guard standards. Recruits receive their uniforms. All recruits are assigned to a company of up to 120 people led by a company commander. The early days of basic are filled with a lot of physical fitness training. Recruits also work on memorizing what the coast guard calls "required knowledge." It includes general orders and customs that all coast guard personnel must adhere to. This required knowledge can be found online, and some recruits begin memorizing it before arriving at basic. Recruits attend academic classes and start learning military customs. As the weeks pass, in addition to classroom work and physical fitness training, recruits learn firefighting, seamanship, and marksmanship.

At the end of the fifth week of basic, recruits get their orders telling them where they will be serving. More training comes later as recruits head into their specialized jobs. Upon graduating from basic training, recruits are ready to serve in the coast guard.

★ A coast guard recruit does push-ups during training as an officer watches.

CHAPTER 4

BOATSWAIN'S MATE

Boatswain's mates operate and navigate the coast guard's boats and cutters. This job is one of the coast guard's enlisted ratings. The word *boatswain*, pronounced "bosun," originates from the Middle English word *bootswein*, in which *boot* meant "boat" and *swein* meant "boy" or "servant." Coast guard boatswain's mates are experts in all areas of deck seamanship and navigation. Outside of officer jobs, boatswain's mate is

38

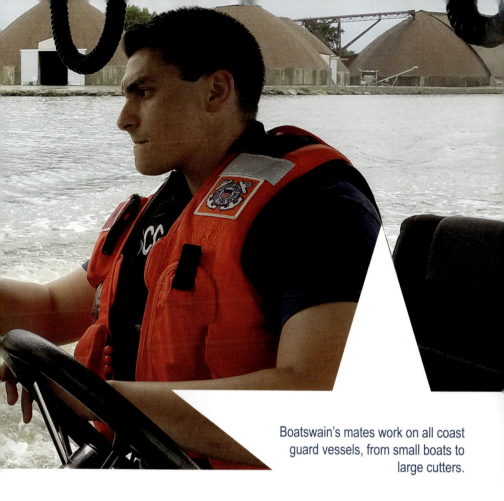

Boatswain's mates work on all coast guard vessels, from small boats to large cutters.

the only coast guard rating where there is the opportunity to command cutters and stations.

"MASTERS OF SEAMANSHIP"

"Boatswain's mates are masters of seamanship," said Senior Chief Petty Officer Todd Stein. "BMs are capable of performing almost any task in connection with deck maintenance, small boat operations, navigation, and supervising all personnel assigned to a ship's work force or small boat station."[1] Because boatswain's mates can perform just about any tasks related to

39

boats and seamanship, they are often described as the most versatile members of the coast guard.

Boatswain's mates are trained in operating the coast guard's complex navigation and operating systems. "A boatswain's mate can trace their job all the way back to the first sailors that took to the sea," said Petty Officer Pete O'Brien. "However, today we incorporate the latest technology and communications equipment. I love the sea, and this job is able to get me out there every day."[2]

As members of the largest career field for enlisted coastguardsmen, boatswain's mates get started with 14 weeks of training at the Coast Guard Training Center in Yorktown, Virginia, where they learn the basics of boat operations.

SURFMEN

Within the boatswain's mate rating, there is an elite community of boat operators called "surfmen." These men and women are skilled at operating boats in the most dangerous conditions. A coast guard coxswain can operate vessels in heavy seas. But only surfmen are allowed to operate boats in dangerous breaking waves.

Being a surfman does not just mean driving boats in challenging surf conditions. Surfmen must also be able to manage the most complex search-and-rescue scenarios that might occur. Becoming a surfman requires years of training in the most difficult weather and surf conditions, learning with the most experienced coast guard boat operators. Only a small number of coast guard members achieve the surfman certification.

This training comes after the basic training they completed when entering the coast guard. During their training in Yorktown, boatswain's mates learn how to be coxswains, or boat drivers. They focus on leadership, law enforcement, and lifesaving skills. Boatswain's mates might later attend advanced training.

Petty Officer Third Class Shannon Eubanks is a boatswain's mate stationed aboard the coast guard cutter *Healy*, a polar icebreaker. In the summer, Eubanks is deployed to the Arctic to assist military and civilian scientists in conducting research in that region. As a boatswain's mate, her job is to pilot the ship's small boats and to stand watch on the ship's bridge. "Military service can be a bit of a challenge," Eubanks

BREAKING ICE

The coast guard is the only branch of the US military that has icebreakers, which are ships that break a channel through the ice on a body of water so that other ships can pass through. Icebreakers are among the coast guard's largest ships. They range in size from 240 feet (73 m) to 420 feet (128 m) in length. They are easy to spot because the main body of the ships are painted bright red, called "icebreaker red," to make them stand out in icy waters.

Like other coast guard ships, boatswain's mates work aboard icebreakers. Some of the coast guard icebreakers are used to conduct scientific research in the coldest regions of the world. Along with the coast guard crew, research scientists travel with these ships. These ships are also used for search and rescue, environmental protection, and law enforcement in remote regions. One of the coast guard icebreakers works to keep the shipping lanes on the Great Lakes open so other ships can pass through during the winter months.[3]

41

said. "At times, you have to take on different personalities you wouldn't normally display. You also have to force yourself to be more responsible because you have a more responsible role."[4]

DEPLOYMENT

Coast guard personnel are assigned to a home base. However, they sometimes leave these home bases for periods of time called deployments. For coastguardsmen assigned to the larger cutters, deployments may last for three months or more. During this time, the cutter and its crew are out on patrol, visiting other ports. For coastguardsmen assigned to smaller cutters and aircraft, the deployments might last just a few days or a few weeks.

Growing up, Eubanks said, she never really considered the military as a career. But once she began to think about what to do after high school, she began to think about military service. She looked at the other branches of the military, but ultimately the coast guard's mission appealed to her. Any person considering the job of boatswain's mate must have strong leadership qualities, physical strength, good hearing, normal color vision, and strong manual dexterity.

Boatswain's mates serve aboard every coast guard cutter. Their work can include patrolling the coasts, operating tugboats in harbors, or being part of search-and-rescue teams. They can also act as federal law enforcement officers. As such, their duties include maritime law enforcement, anti-terrorism efforts, and port security and safety.

★ A coast guard boatswain's mate prepares a heaving line, which is used to pass larger lines to other ships and piers, often to dock a ship.

O'Brien likes the variety that comes with the boatswain's mate job. "The ocean changes every day and so do the challenges that come with that," he said. "A boatswain's mate has to be proficient in all aspects of seamanship."[5]

BOATSWAIN'S MATES TAKE COMMAND

Aboard coastal patrol boats, river tenders, harbor tugs, and small shore units (such as search-and-rescue stations or aids to navigation teams), boatswain's mates can become officers-in-charge. This opportunity for command is unique among the coast guard's enlisted jobs. With the exception of boatswain's mates, the responsibility of commanding a team is typically only for officers.

"I enjoy leadership positions and taking on responsibility, so it was the perfect fit," said Boatswain's Mate Philip Kiley, who serves in the coast guard reserves. "You know being a small service, every member is important to get the mission done. You get a lot of responsibility put on you at a young age."[6] Kiley decided during boot camp that he wanted to pursue the boatswain's mate job. The versatile job with its responsibilities in navigation, small boat operations, and deck maintenance appealed to him.

After life in the coast guard, boatswain's mates can move on to a wide range of civilian jobs. These include jobs as harbormasters, charter boat captains, heavy equipment

MAKING AN IMPACT

Boatswain's mates are called the most versatile members of the coast guard's operational team. They are described as masters of seamanship. Although the boatswain's mate job has been around for a long time, today's boatswain's mates find themselves trained and skilled in all the latest technologies related to seamanship. Boatswain's mates are essential to almost every operation the coast guard undertakes. They are hands-on involved in law enforcement, security operations, and search and rescue. Their expertise in seamanship and skills in navigation keep the coast guard and its vessels running each day.

operators, ship pilots, and port managers, as well as careers in law enforcement and emergency operations management.

TOP FIVE QUESTIONS

★ **WHAT DOES A BOATSWAIN'S MATE DO?**
Boatswain's mates are experts in all areas of operating and navigating the coast guard's boats and cutters.

★ **WHERE DOES A BOATSWAIN'S MATE WORK?**
Boatswain's mates are assigned to almost every US Coast Guard duty station in the United States and overseas. They serve aboard every coast guard cutter.

★ **WHAT KINDS OF BOATS DOES A BOATSWAIN'S MATE WORK ON?**
Boatswain's mates can work aboard a wide variety of vessels, from large cutters to smaller coastal patrol boats.

★ **WHAT SHOULD A PERSON STUDY IN SCHOOL TO BECOME A BOATSWAIN'S MATE?**
The coast guard recommends that young people who want to become boatswain's mates take high school courses in algebra, geometry, and shop.

★ **WHAT QUALIFICATIONS DOES A PERSON NEED FOR THE JOB OF BOATSWAIN'S MATE?**
A coast guard enlistee needs a high school diploma. In some special situations, the coast guard will accept a person with a GED. Boatswain's mates need to be strong leaders who are able to work well on teams and do not mind sometimes performing repetitive tasks. Experience in handling small boats is also useful for young people pursuing a boatswain's mate job.

CHAPTER 5

MARITIME ENFORCEMENT SPECIALIST

Maritime enforcement specialists perform law enforcement and security duties. They protect US ports and waterways, safeguarding them from illegal activity. Their duties

Coast guard maritime enforcement specialists often work in partnership with local law enforcement agencies.

include traditional maritime law enforcement, anti-terrorism efforts, force protection, and port security and safety. This coast guard enlisted rating is relatively new, created in 2010. Before 2010, other coast guard members handled law enforcement duties along with their other work.

After basic training, a maritime enforcement specialist begins with ten weeks of training in Charleston, South Carolina, at the Federal Law Enforcement Training Center. The training program focuses on leadership, military bearing, and the coast guard's core values. Students learn to carry out the coast guard's law enforcement mission of keeping US ports, waterways, and coasts secure; preventing and controlling illegal drug smuggling; keeping US borders secure and enforcing immigration laws; and ensuring that the country is prepared and defended against any hostile attacks. Maritime enforcement specialists also train in force protection, where they learn how to keep coast guard personnel, facilities, and resources safe from attack.

Part of the training is centered on the physical aspects of the maritime enforcement specialist job, such as tactical procedures, handcuffing, and defensive tactics. This instruction prepares the trainees to work as a team in situations where force is required to capture a suspect. Trainees learn first aid techniques for treating life-threatening injuries. As part of anti-terrorism and force protection training, students learn how to conduct

A LOT TO PROTECT

The coast guard is responsible for a very big area of water. The coast guard protects and defends more than 100,000 miles (161,000 km) of US coastline and inland waterways. In addition to the coastline and waterways, the coast guard also protects natural resources in an area of water covering 4.5 million square miles (11.7 million sq km), reaching from north of the Arctic to south of the equator. This area includes ocean waters off the coast of Alaska, the Atlantic and Pacific coasts of the United States, and the waters around some of the islands of the western Pacific.[1]

★ Some maritime enforcement specialists are K-9 handlers, working with dogs that are trained to locate explosives, drugs, or other illegal items.

vehicle inspections and recognize possibilities for preventing terrorist attacks.

Men and women training to be maritime enforcement specialists learn about weapons by spending time on the firing range with pistols, rifles, and shotguns. Petty Officer First Class Jesse Pitrelli is a maritime enforcement specialist and one of the first two active duty coastguardsmen to graduate from the US Army Sniper Course at Fort Benning, Georgia, in 2016. Pitrelli described the value of firearms training for maritime enforcement

CHIEF WARRANT OFFICER AMY BARRINGER

In June 2019, Amy Barringer made history when she became the first active duty female warrant officer in her specialty—maritime enforcement specialist. In the US military, warrant officers are between the enlisted ranks and the officer ranks. They are usually officers who have specialized skills in a technical area.

Barringer's first coast guard job was as a gunner's mate. When the new maritime enforcement specialist rating opened, she moved into that job. She set her sights on becoming a warrant officer. "I applied nine times before I was picked up," she explained. Her persistence paid off. "I'm happy that women have really great opportunities in the coast guard," she said. "I think the coast guard works a little bit harder at breaking stigmas and trying to be inclusive. I feel as though I've always been valued and appreciated."[3]

specialists, who may be put in dangerous situations because of their jobs:

> The instructors are experts in their craft, and many of them have had actual experience overseas executing their mission, so they stressed that life and death can depend on the crossroads between preparation and opportunity. People think that these situations can't arise in the coast guard, but coastguardsmen put themselves in the path of dangerous people on a daily basis. This kind of training is essential for the coast guard to match the growing threats we continue to face on a day-to-day basis all over the world.[2]

TOP PHYSICAL CONDITION

Physical fitness is another important part of training for maritime enforcement specialists. Getting into top physical condition and maintaining that condition is key to success in the job. Maritime enforcement specialists need good stamina and endurance.

Petty Officer First Class Raymond Concepcion stressed the importance of physical fitness in his success as a maritime enforcement specialist. Concepcion described how his job requires him to board ships that are already moving, looking for security violations or other kinds of threats. When Concepcion boards a ship, he and his shipmates attach a ladder to the ship. This ladder can reach 20 to 40 feet (6 to 12 m) up the side of the ship. Wind and waves can make climbing the ladders a serious

MAKING AN IMPACT

Because of the coast guard's unique law enforcement duties, maritime enforcement specialists play a key role in protecting US ports and waters. They guard against any kind of illegal activity, ranging from the smuggling of weapons or drugs to terrorism to maritime law enforcement.

Petty Officer Christopher Hartman, a maritime enforcement specialist, described the importance of his job. "Every day we're actively engaged in law enforcement operations," he said. "We're countering terrorism, we're searching for drug smugglers—whatever it takes to protect our nation's ports and waterways. I can't imagine doing anything else."[4]

51

★ Maritime enforcement specialists must undergo firearms and marksmanship training.

physical challenge. Maritime enforcement specialists must also be able to chase and apprehend fleeing suspects when needed. "If a stowaway is located, you need the stamina to be able to deal with that situation," said Concepcion.[5] He follows a strict workout plan and eats a healthy diet in order to stay in shape for the job.

After leaving the coast guard, maritime enforcement specialists often find jobs in law enforcement at the local, state, or federal level. Their skills in enforcing maritime laws make them strong candidates for jobs in civilian law enforcement. Some maritime enforcement specialists later work in security jobs for private companies.

TOP FIVE QUESTIONS

★ **WHAT DOES A MARITIME ENFORCEMENT SPECIALIST DO?**
Maritime enforcement specialists enforce the law and provide security in US ports and waterways.

★ **WHERE DOES A MARITIME ENFORCEMENT SPECIALIST WORK?**
Maritime enforcement specialists are assigned to coast guard cutters, coast guard police departments, marine safety and security teams, maritime security response teams, coast guard stations, and port security units that are deployed around the world.

★ **WHAT SKILLS DOES MARITIME ENFORCEMENT SPECIALIST TRAINING FOCUS ON?**
Maritime enforcement specialists learn many specific tactics that they use to catch suspects. However, they also learn some more general skills, such as first aid and marksmanship.

★ **WHAT SHOULD A PERSON STUDY IN SCHOOL TO BECOME A MARITIME ENFORCEMENT SPECIALIST?**
To enlist in the coast guard, a person needs a high school diploma. In some special situations, the coast guard will accept a person with a GED. Classes in psychology, sociology, criminal justice, political science, and physical education can be helpful for a person interested in becoming a maritime enforcement specialist.

★ **WHAT SKILLS DOES A PERSON NEED FOR THE JOB OF MARITIME ENFORCEMENT SPECIALIST?**
In a law enforcement job such as maritime enforcement specialist, a person needs the ability to stay calm in high-pressure situations and the willingness to perform potentially dangerous tasks. Being physically fit and having strong leadership skills are also important.

CHAPTER 6

DAMAGE CONTROLMAN

A coast guard damage controlman (DC) excels at a lot of different tasks all rolled into one job. The coast guard describes damage controlmen as "maintenance and emergency repair specialists."[1] These enlisted personnel are responsible for maintaining and repairing a wide range of coast guard equipment. They are also prepared to handle major disasters that might harm a ship or their coast guard colleagues. Petty

54

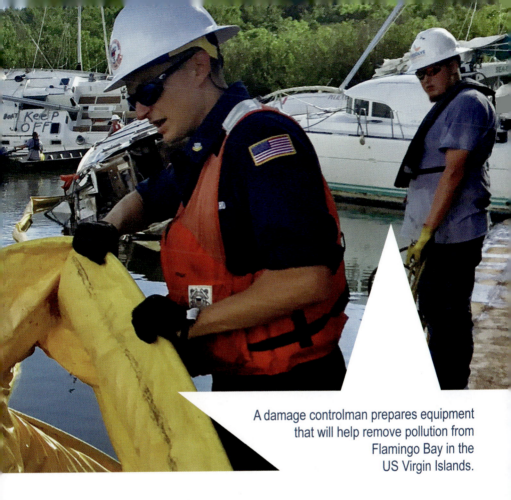

A damage controlman prepares equipment that will help remove pollution from Flamingo Bay in the US Virgin Islands.

Officer Second Class Meghan Richter explained the job, saying, "We are a jack-of-all-trades, with a lot of creativity. On the ship, my job when we leave the pier is to make sure in the event something was to go wrong, everyone knows where to go and how to communicate and combat a casualty."[2]

Damage controlmen handle a range of tasks from repairing plumbing to welding to defending against chemical, biological, or nuclear warfare. A chemical, biological, or nuclear attack would involve an enemy releasing a dangerous substance. A wide

Damage controlmen are trained to fight fires.

range of US military service members are trained in defending against and containing these types of attacks.

Overall, the job of a damage controlman is to keep the coast guard's people, boats, aircraft, and facilities safe and operating well. Sometimes that means fixing things such as broken sewer lines or water lines. Other times it means fighting disasters such as fires or floods.

Firefighting can be especially challenging when a fire breaks out at sea, aboard a ship or on an oil platform. Land-based fire trucks and firefighters cannot get there to help. The coast guard's damage controlmen are often the first people to respond to the fire.

Damage controlmen also train their shipmates to respond safely when disasters like fire or flooding happen aboard a ship.

MAKING AN IMPACT

Damage controlmen's problem-solving skills keep a ship running safely. "We're firefighters, welders, plumbers, carpenters. We're basically the jack-of-all-trades," said Petty Officer First Class Timothy Florez Adams.[3]

Aboard coast guard vessels, damage controlmen ensure that the ship runs safely. "It creates a sense of reward because you know you're making a change, you know you're being useful," DC1 Victor Arcelay said. "And you know you're using the training that you acquired . . . so you know that you're a cog, a moving part of this great machinery that is this cutter."[4]

57

DYING IN THE LINE OF DUTY

Petty Officer Third Class Nathan Bruckenthal was a US Coast Guard damage controlman killed in the Iraq War (2003–2011) on April 24, 2004. He was the first coastguardsman to be killed in the line of duty since the Vietnam War (1954–1975). Bruckenthal served aboard a US Navy vessel in the North Arabian Gulf. He died along with two US Navy sailors when they attempted to board a small boat near an Iraqi oil terminal. When they boarded the boat, a suicide bomber blew up the boat. Bruckenthal was buried in Arlington Cemetery in Arlington, Virginia. In 2018, the coast guard commissioned a new cutter named *Nathan Bruckenthal*.

Richter stresses the importance of this. "It's my job to be a subject matter expert, but I can't fight fires completely by myself—I need to pass my knowledge on so everyone here can work as a team," she said.[5]

REMAIN CALM, THINK QUICKLY

The range of responsibilities for damage controlmen require them to think fast and help each other to fix things and solve problems. "This is a job which, to me, means hard work, and because of that we take care of each other," said Petty Officer Second Class Anthony Pope. "DCs are, in my experience, great people who share information with each other so someone tackling a problem somewhere else can learn from them. This job teaches you to remain calm and think quickly."[6]

Damage controlmen generally serve aboard coast guard vessels. DC1 Victor Arcelay served aboard the coast guard

★ A damage controlman welds aboard the coast guard cutter *Eagle* to repair a part of the ship.

cutter *Active*, an older vessel that was first used in 1966. He described the challenging job of keeping the ship safely running. "I deal with all kinds of repairs, shipboard firefighting, training," Arcelay said. "Basically, I can do anything from welding to carpentry, but I'm neither a licensed welder nor a licensed carpenter. . . . So, imagine you have a ship that's 52, 53 years old, you have to deal with systems that are about the same age. As everything advances, parts become obsolete and chasing down parts or figuring out how to fix what you have available is a challenge. . . . Luckily, here we are, we didn't sink, we didn't catch on fire. Everything's working tip-top."[7]

Damage controlmen are focused on the safety of both their shipmates and the ship. "I care a lot," said Petty Officer First Class Timothy J. Florez Adams. "I care about making sure that when my ship's underway that the safety of the crew is going to happen—that we're well trained, well qualified, that spaces are maintained the way they're supposed to be."[8]

TRAINING AND CAREER INTERESTS

Damage controlmen get started with 15 weeks of training in Yorktown, Virginia. They are trained in a variety of skills including welding, firefighting, carpentry, plumbing, watertight

COAST GUARD CUTTER *EAGLE* SAILS

The coast guard has many cutters and boats outfitted with the latest state-of-the-art technologies. But it also has a sailing ship called the *Eagle*. The coast guard cutter *Eagle* was built in 1936 and is still sailing today. At 295 feet (89.9 m) long, the *Eagle* holds the honor of being the largest active tall sailing ship in the US military.

Cadets from the Coast Guard Academy and people who enter the coast guard through Officer Candidate School spend at least six weeks training aboard the *Eagle*. They learn basic seamanship, navigation, and leadership skills. They also learn skills specific to certain jobs, such as damage control. The coast guard describes the *Eagle* as a "floating classroom" for future officers where they learn the importance of working together as crew members.[10]

closure maintenance, chemical-biological-radiological warfare defense, and shipboard damage control.

"Whether you decide to be a DC for five, 15, 20, or 30 years, the one thing anyone should take away from the DC [job] is that it's fun and challenging," said Master Chief William Jette. "There are a lot of opportunities and you're going to have a real great time performing all of the different jobs while doing the coast guard's missions."[9]

Damage controlman can be a good career choice for a person who enjoys problem-solving, tinkering, building, or repairing. A young person considering the damage controlman rating may have interests in construction and repair work. Hands-on experience or training in welding, carpentry, plumbing, or firefighting is helpful for a person entering this job. After leaving the coast guard, damage controlmen often find civilian jobs as welders, plumbers, carpenters, pipe fitters, firefighters, trade school teachers, or construction foremen.

TOP FIVE QUESTIONS

★ **WHAT DOES A DAMAGE CONTROLMAN DO?**
The damage controlman rating includes a wide range of tasks from firefighting to plumbing repair to welding to detecting nuclear warfare materials.

★ **WHERE DOES A DAMAGE CONTROLMAN WORK?**
Damage controlmen usually serve aboard cutters. They are stationed at coast guard locations across the United States, including in Alaska, Hawaii, and Puerto Rico.

★ **WHAT SKILLS DOES COAST GUARD DAMAGE CONTROLMAN TRAINING FOCUS ON?**
Damage controlmen are trained in carpentry, welding, plumbing, firefighting aboard ships, and chemical-biological-radiological warfare defense.

★ **WHAT SHOULD A PERSON STUDY IN SCHOOL TO BECOME A DAMAGE CONTROLMAN?**
School courses in math and chemistry are useful preparation for a damage controlman. Also, courses or experience in carpentry, welding, or plumbing are useful to people who want to work as damage controlmen.

★ **WHAT PERSONAL SKILLS ARE USEFUL FOR THE JOB OF DAMAGE CONTROLMAN?**
Damage controlmen must be able to stay calm in stressful situations and make smart decisions quickly. They should also be willing to risk danger to help others.

63

CHAPTER 7

AVIATOR

Coast guard aviators are trained to fly the aircraft (helicopters and airplanes) that the US Coast Guard uses in its work. All of these pilots are officers. The coast guard flies five types of aircraft, which are spread among its 24 air stations. Aviators fly to support all of the coast guard's missions, including search and rescue, drug interdiction, protecting the environment,

A coast guard aviator in Hawaii examines a helicopter that belongs to the Honolulu Fire Department.

and anti-terrorism work. They work with federal, state, and local agencies.

Helicopter pilot Lieutenant Commander Tom Huntley described the importance of the work he does by talking about a mission he flew to rescue three sailors who sent out a Mayday signal. "We brought them back and got them to land again," he said. "The gentleman said to me, 'I never thought I would see solid earth again.' They thought that they were gone. So, to bring them back from 30-foot [9 m] seas, having been rolled a

COAST GUARD AIRCRAFT

The coast guard has approximately 200 fixed-wing and rotary-wing aircraft.[3] A fixed-wing aircraft is an airplane. A rotary-wing aircraft is a helicopter. Most of the aircraft are used to support the coast guard's role in homeland security, so they are armed with weapons. The aircraft are used for jobs ranging from surveillance to rescue to disaster response to transportation. Because the coast guard's fleet of aircraft is small compared with the aircraft fleets of other military branches, many of the aircraft are outfitted to carry out a range of tasks, not just one single job. For example, the MH-60T helicopter is outfitted with night-vision equipment that allows crew members to perform search-and-rescue missions, homeland security missions, and law enforcement missions. The HC-144A maritime patrol aircraft can perform search-and-rescue missions or transport missions carrying personnel and cargo.

couple times in their sailboat, and having given up on the idea that they were going to be rescued, bringing them back was pretty amazing."[1]

The coast guard has approximately 800 pilots, along with about 2,500 enlisted people who work with the pilots providing support as the aircrew.[2] Perhaps surprisingly, the coast guard actually has more pilots than ship drivers. These pilots play an essential role in the coast guard's search-and-rescue missions and in humanitarian relief during storms or other disasters. Over the course of their coast guard careers, aviators may fly different types of aircraft.

PATHWAYS TO PILOT JOBS

Some coastguardsmen attend flight training immediately after they graduate from the Coast Guard Academy. Up to 10 percent of each graduating class (approximately 20 cadets) heads directly to flight training.[4] Others are selected for flight school within three years.

College students who are in the coast guard's College Student Pre-Commissioning Initiative (CSPI) scholarship program can apply for a guaranteed flight school position. The path from the CSPI program into flight school is called the Wilks' Flight Initiative (WiFI) program.

AVIATORS TO ASTRONAUTS

Two coast guard aviators have become astronauts for the National Aeronautics and Space Administration (NASA). NASA selected coast guard Commander Bruce Melnick for the astronaut program in 1987. He became the first coastguardsman to fly in space. Melnick flew on the space missions STS-41 in 1990 and STS-49 in 1992.

NASA selected coast guard Captain Daniel Burbank for the astronaut program in 1988, making him the second coast guard pilot to fly in space. He was a mission specialist on STS-106 in 2000 and STS-115 in 2006.

Burbank said his coast guard training helped him prepare for being an astronaut. "It's the best background in the world," he said. "To be a team player; to understand how to operate in the craziest, dangerous, hazardous conditions; to do a great humanitarian mission; and probably the best training ground I ever could have asked for to then fly in space."[5]

★ The coast guard has ships that are equipped for aviators to land aircraft.

Coast guard, navy, and marine corps pilots all begin their training at the Naval Air Station in Pensacola, Florida. Once coast guard pilots complete their basic flight training, they head to the Coast Guard Aviation Training Center in Mobile, Alabama, for more training specific to coast guard aircraft. When aviators complete their training in Mobile, they are designated as copilots and report to their first coast guard air station to begin work.

Pilots from other branches of the military can become coast guard aviators. They first attend the Direct Commission Officer course in New London, Connecticut, for four weeks. Then they head to the Coast Guard Aviation Training Center in Mobile. Aviators who enter the coast guard through the Direct

Commission Officer route are committed to serve in active duty for five years.

AVIATION JOBS FOR ENLISTED PERSONNEL

While all coast guard pilots are officers, there are aviation jobs for enlisted personnel. An aviation maintenance technician (AMT) maintains coast guard aircraft and serves as a crew member aboard the aircraft. AMTs serve in positions such as flight engineer, flight mechanic, precision marksman, loadmaster, dropmaster, and basic aircrewman. Precision marksmen are highly skilled in shooting. A loadmaster is responsible for the loading, transport, and unloading of cargo. A dropmaster is responsible for any cargo that is air-dropped from the aircraft.

WOMEN IN THE COAST GUARD

In 1918, the first uniformed women began to serve in the US Coast Guard. Myrtle Hazard was one of these early female coastguardsmen. She was a telegraph operator, serving during World War I (1914–1918). In 1957, Virginia Schroeder became the first woman in the coast guard to qualify for the Expert Pistol Medal, an award for great marksmanship. In 1976, the first women were admitted to the Coast Guard Academy. But it was not until 1977 that Janna Lambine became the first woman designated as a coast guard aviator. Lambine was the first female coast guard aviator and the first female coast guard helicopter pilot. She flew the HH-3 helicopter. Lambine served with US forces in Operation Desert Storm, fighting against Iraq during the Gulf War (1990–1991). She retired from the coast guard reserves in 2000.

★ Coast guard aircrew members prepare a helicopter for deployment.

Avionics electrical technicians troubleshoot and repair complex avionics and electrical systems on coast guard aircraft. They also serve as members of the aircrew, filling positions such as navigator, flight mechanic, radio operator, sensor systems operator, and basic aircrewman.

Aviation Maintenance Technician Nicole Rivas works on MH-65 Dolphin helicopters. "I knew I wanted to choose a specialty that would give me opportunities to do things that I would never have been able to do outside the coast guard," she said. "Aviation obviously stood out to me for that, and the AMT specialty interested me because it was something I hadn't done before. Going from zero mechanical knowledge or experience (I had never even changed the oil in my car before), to fixing and flying in helicopters, seemed like exactly the type of challenge I was looking for in the coast guard."[6]

Ashley Laugavitz's high school science teacher suggested that she consider a career in the coast guard. When she enlisted, she heard about the AMT job. Laugavitz went on to work with coast guard helicopters. "It sparked my interest because I've

MAKING AN IMPACT

Whether they are flying search-and-rescue missions to save people in danger, flying law enforcement missions to keep the United States safe, or flying missions to monitor and protect the marine environment, coast guard pilots play a critical role in safeguarding US coasts, ports, and waterways.

Angel Hughes, a coast guard aviator, earned her private pilot's license while in high school. She joined the coast guard after graduating from college and went on to become an aircraft commander and military instructor pilot. Hughes flies the C-144 aircraft that the coast guard uses for search and rescue, logistics operations (moving troops and supplies), and law enforcement missions. Hughes is proud to be a coast guard aviator. "Every day I'm on duty I never know what I'm going to get," she said. "I'm proud of being a coast guard aviator, and standing the duty."[7]

71

always enjoyed working with my hands and taking on new challenges," she said. "I also loved the fact that we would get to fix and fly in helicopters, which is unlike any other specialty in the coast guard or any other branch for that matter."[8]

Analise Caveness is an AMT who works on the coast guard's C-130J Super Hercules aircraft. She considered a variety of coast guard jobs before deciding that working as a member of the flight crew was the right choice for her. "My first station was a 378-foot [115 m] cutter out of Hawaii. I got to see pretty much all of the coast guard's specialties. I was up in the air about what specialty I wanted to choose. It wasn't until I got to talk to the flight crew on one of the deployments that I thought, 'Ok, I could do this for 20 years.' I've been happy with it ever since."[9] Whether it's piloting the coast guard's aircraft or working as a member of the flight crew, many people find coast guard aviation to be an enjoyable and fulfilling career path.

TOP FIVE QUESTIONS

★ **WHAT DOES AN AVIATOR DO?**
Aviators fly the coast guard's airplanes and helicopters.

★ **WHERE DOES AN AVIATOR WORK?**
Aviators are assigned to coast guard air stations. Helicopter pilots can get deployed to large coast guard cutters that are equipped with a flight deck.

★ **CAN ENLISTED COAST GUARD MEMBERS BECOME AVIATORS?**
No, all coast guard aviators must be officers. However, an enlisted member who has a bachelor's degree can work toward becoming an officer. Additionally, there are other coast guard jobs related to aviation that do not involve flying aircraft. These include enlisted coastguardsmen who repair and maintain aircraft.

★ **WHAT SHOULD A PERSON STUDY IN SCHOOL TO BECOME AN AVIATOR?**
Students wanting to become aviators can help prepare themselves by taking math and physics courses in high school.

★ **WHAT QUALIFICATIONS DOES A PERSON NEED FOR THE JOB OF AVIATOR?**
To qualify for the coast guard's flight training, a person must have a bachelor's degree and be commissioned as a coast guard officer. Aviators also need to have self-confidence, strong awareness of what is going on around them, attention to detail, the ability to stay calm under stress, and strong communication skills.

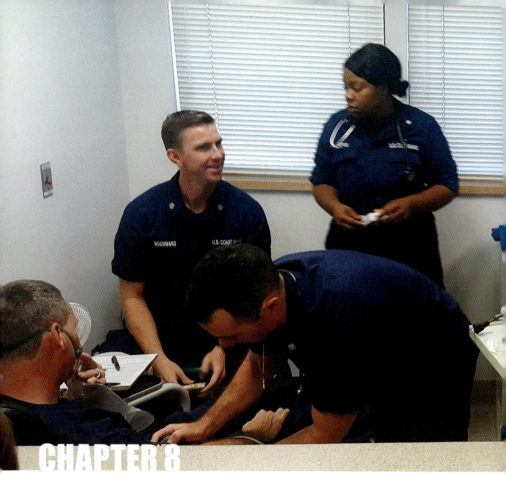

CHAPTER 8

PHARMACIST

The US Coast Guard offers a wide range of job opportunities in the medical field. The job of pharmacist is one of these career paths. Within the officer ranks, the coast guard also offers medical careers for physicians, health services officers, environmental health officers, dentists, and clinical and rehabilitation therapists.

Coast guard pharmacists work closely with other medical personnel.

Pharmacists work at coast guard clinics caring for patients, monitoring new drugs, and helping in public health emergencies. Pharmacists often must work together with other coast guard medical providers. Coast guard Pharmacist Commander Benjamin C. Keller said, "I appreciate the collaborative practice aspect of pharmacy in the coast guard; it's really [about] getting to work with the providers and knowing your [doctors]," he said. "They really value what pharmacy brings to the table."[1]

MASTERS OF MULTITASKING

Pharmacists provide medical and dental care in clinics and sick bays for more than 41,000 active duty coast guard personnel. Many of these are small clinics where there is one pharmacist. "Most of the coast guard pharmacies are pretty small, so you get to do it all," Keller said.[2] One responsibility of pharmacists in these small clinics is to guide the work of health services technicians. Health services technician is a coast guard enlisted job similar to the job of a paramedic in the civilian world.

The variety of work at these clinics requires coast guard pharmacists to multitask. "No two days are the same," said Commander Aaron P. Middlekauff, a coast guard pharmacist. "One day you could be doing a sick bay inspection aboard a cutter, the next day [teaching] students and enlisted medical staff, the next day

HEALTH SERVICES TECHNICIANS

Most coast guard medical jobs are in the officer ranks, and they require at least four years of college, plus medical school training. However, the job of health services technician is in the enlisted ranks. These technicians attend an intense five months of training in Petaluma, California. This training includes lectures, labs, and clinical work. Students learn about anatomy, nursing skills, wound repair, and many other topics. They also take a basic course in emergency medical technician training. Once they complete the training, health services technicians work alongside doctors, dentists, and pharmacists. They perform diagnostic tests, X-rays, lab tests, and minor surgical procedures. They prescribe medicine and administer immunizations.

disaster relief. In a way, the coast guard is like a small town, where the mayor might also be a firefighter and a local business owner. But then we're not just [in the United States]. The coast guard operates around the globe all the way down to the Caribbean and as far as southwest Asia."[3]

Middlekauff described the kind of person who works well in this environment. "They should have served in patient care and have administrative experience in order to comfortably navigate the multifaceted pharmacist role within the coast guard," he said. "The work isn't a deep-dive into any particular specialty care,

MAKING AN IMPACT

Pharmacists are a vital part of the US Coast Guard medical team. Partnering with other coast guard health-care professionals, pharmacists ensure that all coast guard personnel have the medicines they need to stay healthy and strong.

Coast guard service members do important jobs and work in challenging situations, sometimes overseas. Their health and well-being are key as they strive to do their jobs well. Pharmacists are important team members in ensuring that all coast guard personnel stay healthy and ready to serve.

Captain Pamela Stewart-Kuhn, a pharmacist, said, "Of course, my patients want their medicine, but I also know that my interactions with my patients are providing a service to others, whether through providing resources and information, providing a kind word of encouragement, or simply just listening. After all, our primary job is service, not just to the coast guard, but to our patients."[4]

All coast guard pharmacists are officers. ★

and requires being able to facilitate a multitude of various duties and tasks, often simultaneously."[5]

An important piece of balancing everything is the pharmacist's work with health service technicians, Keller said. "You rely on your techs a lot and pump a lot of advanced knowledge into them," he said. "We expect a lot out of our techs."[6]

Coast guard pharmacists are a part of the US Public Health Service (USPHS) Commissioned Corps. The USPHS is a part of a larger federal government agency, the Department of Health and Human Services. USPHS pharmacy officers serve in a variety of federal agencies and programs. The coast

US PUBLIC HEALTH SERVICE

The coast guard is not the only place where US Public Health Service Commissioned Corps pharmacists serve. They also work for federal agencies such as the Indian Health Service, Food and Drug Administration, Federal Bureau of Prisons, National Institutes of Health, and Centers for Disease Control and Prevention.

The mission of the USPHS is to promote public health in the United States. The USPHS offers a program for students that allows them to serve their country while they finish their education. The Junior Commissioned Officer Student Training and Extern Program is a competitive program for college students in fields such as pharmacy, nursing, environmental health, and engineering. Students are paid to work in their field during their breaks from school. Then when they graduate, they have the opportunity to become full-time USPHS commissioned officers and work for the coast guard or another federal agency.

guard is just one among many federal agencies where USPHS pharmacists can serve. When USPHS pharmacists are assigned to the coast guard, they attend officer training and take part in field exercises and classroom training to learn about being a military officer. Coast guard doctors and dentists are also part of the USPHS Commissioned Corps.

Since coastguardsmen can be sent out to other countries on missions, such as keeping international ports secure, one essential part of a coast guard pharmacist's job is keeping up with vaccines and other necessary travel medicines. "Being military related, we have to always make sure that everybody's vaccines are up to date and everybody's available for deployment," Keller said.[7]

TOP FIVE QUESTIONS

★ **WHAT DOES A COAST GUARD PHARMACIST DO?**
Pharmacists prescribe medicines, care for and advise patients, monitor new drugs, and help in public health emergencies.

★ **WHERE DOES A PHARMACIST WORK?**
Coast guard pharmacists work at coast guard clinics. Many of these clinics are small, with one pharmacist working there.

★ **CAN ENLISTED COAST GUARD MEMBERS BECOME PHARMACISTS?**
No, pharmacist is an officer position in the coast guard. However, an enlisted member who has a bachelor's degree can work to become an officer. Additionally, enlisted coast guard personnel who want to work in health care can pursue the job of health services technician.

★ **WHAT QUALIFICATIONS DOES A PERSON NEED FOR THE JOB OF PHARMACIST?**
To become a coast guard pharmacist, a person must earn a bachelor of science or doctor of pharmacy degree from a program accredited by the American Council on Pharmaceutical Education.

★ **WHAT SHOULD A PERSON WHO IS INTERESTED IN BECOMING A PHARMACIST STUDY IN HIGH SCHOOL?**
Students who want to become pharmacists should take high school courses in biology, chemistry, physics, and calculus in order to best prepare themselves for college.

CHAPTER 9

AVIATION SURVIVAL TECHNICIAN

When storms whip up bad weather near the water, most people seek shelter in a safe, dry place. But US Coast Guard rescue swimmers are trained to head out into storms to rescue people who are drowning. Coast guard rescue swimmers

Coast guard rescue swimmers jump out of helicopters to help people in dangerous areas that are hard to reach any other way.

save civilians in dangerous situations such as floods, hurricanes, or boating accidents.

The official coast guard name for this job is aviation survival technician (AST). But people usually call them "rescue swimmers," which well describes the important job they do. Like the coast guard, the US Navy also has rescue swimmers, but its swimmers are generally tasked with saving downed pilots in combat situations rather than saving civilians, which is what coast guard swimmers do. Coast guard rescue swimmers have

BIRTH OF THE RESCUE SWIMMER PROGRAM

The coast guard's rescue swimmer program was born out of a tragedy in 1983. A ship called *Marine Electric* sunk during a winter storm on February 12 that year. As the ship sank off the Virginia coast, crew members radioed for help. A coast guard helicopter soon arrived to find 34 crew members of the *Marine Electric* in the water, struggling to survive. The pilot positioned the helicopter over the crew members, and the helicopter flight mechanic lowered the rescue basket to the water's surface. But the crew members were so cold from being in the frigid waters that they could not climb into the basket. Despite the crew members being alive in the water when the helicopter arrived, only three of the 34 crew members could be saved. Following that tragic loss of life, the US Congress directed the coast guard in 1984 to establish a rescue swimming program. By 1985, the first coast guard rescue swimmers had been trained and were on the job.

plucked people from rooftops, cliffs, glaciers, caves, and raging waters. Their job is to save lives. The rescue swimmers' motto is "So others may live."

A SPECIAL OPS JOB

In the military, special operations are the unusual missions carried out by elite forces who are specially trained. Famously, the Army Green Berets and the Navy SEALs are special operations units. In the coast guard, the rescue swimmer career is considered a special operations job. Rescue swimmers are well prepared. Men and women who are accepted into the coast guard's rescue swimmer program are physically and mentally strong, and, of course, they are excellent swimmers. Even so, the coast guard rescue swimmer school is among the toughest special operations schools in the military, and the dropout rate is high. Only about half of the people who begin the training to become rescue swimmers graduate from the program. Aviation Survival Technician Erin Custer described the challenge of rescue swimmer training, saying, "It's putting a lot of stress on you physically and mentally to make sure you can handle the stress because when you're out there in the real coast guard, you're out there by yourself."[1]

SARA FAULKNER: THE COAST GUARD'S FIRST FEMALE RESCUE SWIMMER

The coast guard rescue swimmer program was created in 1984. From the beginning, both men and women were allowed to attend the intensely challenging rescue swimmer school. Sara Faulkner made history in 2000 when she became the first woman to graduate from the coast guard's rescue swimmer training. (Prior to Faulkner passing the coast guard course, two women had successfully completed the navy's rescue swimmer course.)

Faulkner saved many lives during her career. During Hurricane Katrina, she and her aircrew rescued 48 people in one night. "It's an awesome job, and adventurous," Faulkner said. "I've been to the South Pole, done an important job, but I wouldn't candy-coat it." As a woman in the military, Faulkner's career path was not always easy. "[At] every single station I have had to fight to be treated equally," she said.[2]

★ Rescue swimmers train in swimming pool simulations as well as in the field.

Rescue swimmer training consists of training on land and in the water. Students do exercises such as push-ups, rope climbing, and kettlebell training to stretch their endurance. In the water, they swim sprints and long distances—500 yards (457 m) and 2,000 yards (1,829 m). They also swim and tread water with weights attached. Rescue swimmer training also includes practice rescuing people in a large pool where wind and rain machines simulate conditions the swimmers will experience in stormy ocean rescues.

Only the most calm and confident rescue swimmer candidates successfully navigate the training and go on to become coast guard rescue swimmers. "The most valuable thing I learned during my training—that I would not have learned otherwise—is that when I am underwater, and my oxygen-deprived lungs begin lurching for air, I'm a good minute away from being in real trouble," said retired rescue swimmer Mario Vittone. "How that translated into safety happened over a year later, on a case that had me underwater longer than I wanted. What would panic me

MAKING AN IMPACT

Coast guard aviation survival technicians are highly skilled and are trained to perform rescue work in severe weather conditions. The people who work as coast guard rescue swimmers take great pride in their jobs. "Holding the title of an AST is an honor because many people try, and not very many succeed. I just feel privileged," said Petty Officer Third Class Evan Gallant.[3]

For a stranded boater or a person struggling to stay above floodwaters, a rescue swimmer brings hope. "Becoming a helicopter rescue swimmer is much more difficult than actually being one (most of the time)," said retired rescue swimmer Mario Vittone, "but for those who make it through the training, their job becomes one of delivering hope."[4]

87

before the school (lurching for air) instead calmed me down. 'You're okay, plenty of time,' I thought."[5]

CONSTANTLY TRAINING

Even after they complete the swimmer school training, rescue swimmers spend hours and hours practicing for rescues. They do this so that when someone is in danger, the rescue swimmers are ready to head out into the water. "It's a job that takes focus, dedication, and humility," said Petty Officer Matthew O'Dell. "AST's train constantly, right from day one. And not everyone makes the cut. I remember some of those early days [training] in the pool as some of the toughest in my life. It was humbling."[6]

Those who graduate from rescue swimmer school are sent on to emergency medical technician training before they join a helicopter crew where they will put their search-and-rescue skills to work. Once rescue swimmers are assigned to their first unit, they devote months to learning the systems and functions of the helicopters. They become important members of the helicopter crew.

Over the course of their careers, rescue swimmers continue to train and attend school to keep their skills in top shape. One option for this is the Advanced Helicopter Rescue School. This program teaches rescue swimmers how to perform cliff rescues. They also train inside caves and on wet rocks along the

★ Rescue swimmers work in all kinds of extreme conditions, including icy waters.

shoreline, where the helicopter cannot go. Rescue swimmers must understand how swirling water moves in caves and around large rocks. They practice swimming in rough seas with heavy waves, learning how to tow a person through that kind

89

of dangerous water. They also practice the teamwork required between the helicopter pilot, the crew, and the rescue swimmer when working in these rough, unpredictable seas.

DRESSED FOR THE WEATHER

Just like their special training, rescue swimmers' gear is important, too. They wear harnesses that hold supplies such as a light, a knife, a locator beacon, and a radio. That harness is also a lifeline. It connects the swimmer to the hoist that lifts him or her out of the water and back to the helicopter. The rescue swimmer's head is protected by a helmet, mask, and snorkel. For cold-weather rescues, swimmers wear three layers of special long underwear with a suit on top to keep them dry. When rescue swimmers are not out on rescue missions, they carefully tend to the maintenance and repair of their rescue and survival equipment. It is essential that all of their gear is ready to go at a moment's notice when a call for help comes in.

TOP FIVE QUESTIONS

★ **WHAT DOES AN AVIATION SURVIVAL TECHNICIAN DO?**
Aviation survival technicians rescue people in danger, especially danger in and around the water. While most of their work involves rescuing people from water, they also rescue people from rugged terrain and even building rooftops, such as during a flood or fire.

★ **WHERE DOES AN AVIATION SURVIVAL TECHNICIAN WORK?**
Aviation survival technicians are assigned to coast guard air stations in the United States, including in Puerto Rico.

★ **WHAT DO AVIATION SURVIVAL TECHNICIANS DO WHEN THEY ARE NOT SWIMMING?**
Aviation survival technicians are important members of the helicopter aircrew. They are trained to work with parachutes, emergency flotation devices, protective clothing, and various helicopter systems, such as those used for cargo delivery.

★ **WHAT SHOULD A PERSON STUDY IN SCHOOL TO BECOME AN AVIATION SURVIVAL TECHNICIAN?**
High school courses in algebra, geometry, and machinery are all helpful for students who are interested in becoming rescue swimmers. These subjects are related to the skills required to use the coast guard's helicopter systems and gear. Participating in sports that require intense physical conditioning is also beneficial.

★ **WHAT QUALIFICATIONS DOES A PERSON NEED FOR THE JOB OF AVIATION SURVIVAL TECHNICIAN?**
Advanced strength, flexibility, and endurance are key for rescue swimmers. Having strong confidence in the water is essential. Additionally, as with all coast guard positions, a high school diploma is required. In some special situations, the coast guard may accept a person with a GED.

CHAPTER 10

MARINE SCIENCE TECHNICIAN

C oast guard marine science technicians work to ensure that the marine environment—oceans, bays, rivers, and wetlands—along the US coastlines is safe and secure. They protect the water from oil and other hazardous pollution. The job requires constant vigilance. Petty Officer First Class Jeff

A coast guard marine science technician, *left*, and a Texas state government worker monitor oil spill cleanup efforts in November 2019.

Gregg, a marine science technician who worked as a hazardous waste coordinator at the coast guard base in Honolulu, Hawaii, described his job of keeping water clean in this way: "We keep the black stuff out of the blue stuff."[1]

Marine science technicians protect US waters by conducting safety inspections and enforcing regulations that prevent pollution in the water. They inspect American and foreign vessels to make sure they are following regulations to keep the crews, the ports, and the water safe and secure. The marine

93

PROTECTING THE ENVIRONMENT

Protecting the environment has been an important part of the coast guard's job for many years. When an oil spill occurs, it can be deadly for fish, shellfish, birds, and marine mammals—everything that lives in the rivers and oceans. For almost 200 years, the US Coast Guard has played a vital role in protecting the marine environment. For example, when the Deepwater Horizon oil spill happened in 2010, it released 210 million gallons (795 million L) of crude oil into the Gulf of Mexico. (Deepwater Horizon was the name of the offshore drilling rig where an explosion and spill occurred.) The Deepwater Horizon spill was massive. Its volume equaled that of almost 90 percent of all the oil spills that had occurred in US waters over the past 40 years put together. The coast guard played a leading role in containing and cleaning up the Deepwater Horizon spill. The coast guard's strong role in protecting marine environments continues today.[3]

science technician job involves both prevention (to keep pollution from happening) and response (when pollution does occur).

Petty Officer First Class Forrest PhiferSpens, who serves as a marine science technician in the coast guard reserve, said:

> *I respond to releases of oil and hazardous materials into the harbors and supervise their cleanup. . . . I also work with local facilities to ensure they follow safe work practices to prevent accidents and discharges. Marine science technicians help prevent incidents that impact the local community . . . which keeps people safe and the harbor working. Our primary goals are to keep people safe and our local waters clean.*[2]

SKILLS AND TRAINING

Many people who enter the marine science technician job are interested in STEM (science, technology, engineering, and math) subjects. Gregg was once assigned to a first responder team for pollution incidents such as offshore oil spills, and he enjoyed that way of working in a STEM career field. "STEM doesn't mean being stuck in a lab," he said. "You can be as active as you want to be."[4] In addition to having strong STEM skills, marine science technicians must pay close attention to details and be highly flexible and consistent. Prior training or experience working in environmental sciences is helpful, too.

MAKING AN IMPACT

When pollution is allowed into rivers, bays, and oceans, it harms all the plant and animal life in and around the water. Pollution also affects humans who live, work, and play near the water. Marine science technicians protect US waters from pollution by oil and other hazardous materials. In their daily tasks, marine science technicians ensure that ships on US waterways and commercial companies along the waterfront are following the rules for keeping the water clean. In the case of a disaster, man-made or natural, marine science technicians are key team members in the coast guard's response. "Every day we work together to ensure maritime safety and security," said Petty Officer Kira Adams, a marine science technician. "From busy ports to pristine shorelines, we protect America's natural resources from hazardous materials and international violators. I take pride in keeping our nation's waters clean and our mariners safe."[5]

95

Petty Officer Kira Adams described a couple of examples of what a "normal day" in her job as a marine science technician might look like. "Yesterday I was on scene with a tank ship who spilled 200 gallons [760 L] of crude oil near an environmentally sensitive area," she said. "I was overseeing a cleanup crew who placed a containment [barrier] to ensure the protection of the wildlife. Earlier today I was part of a team that examined a commuter ferry to ensure the safe voyage for passengers and crew."[6]

Marine science technicians start by attending twelve weeks of school in Yorktown, Virginia. There, they learn how to investigate oil and hazardous material pollution incidents and supervise pollution cleanup operations. The training school also teaches marine science

AIM SUMMER PROGRAM

Some high school students thinking about college might wonder whether the Coast Guard Academy is the right choice for them. The Academy Introduction Mission (AIM) program helps students make that decision. AIM is a one-week summer program for students entering their senior year of high school. It introduces students to the Coast Guard Academy. Ajia, a student who attended AIM, said, "Over the week I learned a lot, not just about the coast guard, but about myself. It gave me a taste of what my life would be like [during coast guard training] and it was a good test to see how I would do under pressure."[7] Students experience military discipline, physical training, team building, and leadership development. Sidney, another student who attended AIM, said, "AIM taught me to be a leader of character and showed me that I am capable of so much more than I thought I could be."[8]

★ A marine science technician helps a pelican covered in oil.

technicians how to perform proper inspections as a way to prevent spills from happening. They learn how to perform commercial waterfront facility and security inspections. They also learn the skills needed for conducting safety and security inspections on foreign vessels that are entering US waters. Marine science technicians might find themselves working with ship captains to make sure their boats are following federal rules and regulations regarding pollution control and prevention.

Before Petty Officer First Class Sean Carrillo entered the coast guard, he said, "I wanted to do something bigger than myself. I wanted to be a part of a team, part of a group. I wanted that kind of comradery. I aspired to do something in law enforcement or with the fire department."[9] Carrillo found a job that matched his desire for enforcing the law when he entered the coast guard and was assigned to the marine science technician rating. After serving in the coast guard, marine science technicians often find civilian jobs working to protect the marine environment, handling hazardous materials, inspecting ships, or responding to hazardous material spills.

COAST GUARD CAREERS

The US Coast Guard offers a wide range of career choices. And, like the job of marine science technician, many other coast guard careers offer training and skills that can be applied later to civilian jobs. Young people with a desire to serve their country may be interested in a career with the coast guard.

Some of the jobs, like the boatswain's mate, date back to the days when sailors first sailed the seas. Other jobs, like the maritime enforcement specialist, are relatively new, created to support the coast guard's growing role in anti-terrorism and law enforcement. For young people to whom rescuing people in distress, protecting US ports and waterways, or caring for the environment sounds appealing, the coast guard offers many opportunities.

TOP FIVE QUESTIONS

★ **WHAT DOES A MARINE SCIENCE TECHNICIAN DO?**
Marine science technicians guard US waters against pollution.

★ **WHERE DOES A MARINE SCIENCE TECHNICIAN WORK?**
Marine science technicians are stationed at coast guard shore-based locations. They also work at the coast guard's Marine Safety Lab and the International Ice Patrol, both of which are located in New London, Connecticut.

★ **WHAT IS A TYPICAL DAY FOR A MARINE SCIENCE TECHNICIAN?**
The marine science technician rating offers a lot of variety. A workday might include boarding and inspecting ships from foreign countries, working to clean up a pollution spill, inspecting barges, or enforcing security in a port.

★ **WHAT SHOULD A PERSON STUDY IN HIGH SCHOOL TO BECOME A MARINE SCIENCE TECHNICIAN?**
Science and math classes in high school are beneficial for students who want to be marine science technicians. Specific courses or work experience in the environmental sciences also help.

★ **WHAT QUALIFICATIONS DOES A PERSON NEED FOR THE JOB OF MARINE SCIENCE TECHNICIAN?**
A college degree is not required for a person to become a marine science technician. However, to enlist in the coast guard, a person needs a high school diploma. In some situations, the coast guard will accept a person with a GED.

ESSENTIAL FACTS

US COAST GUARD HISTORY

★ 1790: On August 4, the US government begins building the ten vessels called cutters that eventually become the Revenue Cutter Service.

★ 1915: The Revenue Cutter Service and Life-Saving Service merge to form the US Coast Guard.

★ 1939: The Lighthouse Service is transferred to the coast guard.

★ 1946: The Bureau of Marine Inspection and Navigation is transferred to the coast guard.

★ 1967: The coast guard is transferred from the US Department of the Treasury to the US Department of Transportation.

★ 2003: The coast guard is transferred from the US Department of Transportation to the US Department of Homeland Security.

★ 2010: The coast guard plays a leading role in cleaning up the massive Deepwater Horizon oil spill in the Gulf of Mexico.

US COAST GUARD ORGANIZATION

The coast guard is one of six US military services. It is unique among the military services because it is part of both the Department of Defense and the Department of Homeland Security. It has about 41,000 active duty members. The coast guard's job is to provide "maritime safety, security, and environmental stewardship in US ports and waterways."

CAREER MOVES
How can you prepare for a career in the US Coast Guard?
- ★ Take relevant high school classes such as math and science.
- ★ Stay in shape—physical exercise and conditioning are key for anyone pursuing a military career.
- ★ Think about what it means to be a team player, a key concept in military life. (High school band, sports teams, and clubs are all places to develop teamwork and leadership skills.)
- ★ Visit the GoCoastGuard.com web page to learn more about coast guard careers.
- ★ Go online and research the Armed Services Vocational Aptitude Battery (ASVAB) to prepare for taking the military entrance exam.

IMPACT ON SOCIETY
From search-and-rescue work to port security to drug interdiction to protecting the environment, the US Coast Guard helps make the United States a safer and more secure place. For a young person who wants to be part of a team doing that kind of work, the coast guard offers many different career opportunities. Many coastguardsmen find their work fulfilling. They understand the great importance of their work saving lives, keeping US waters clean from pollution, and protecting the country from any threats that may come through seaports.

QUOTE
"The coast guard really did appeal to me, partially because it entailed being part of the military combined with the humanitarian and lifesaving mission."

—*US Coast Guard Lieutenant Commander Tom Huntley*

GLOSSARY

aptitude
A natural ability to do something or learn something.

avionics
Electronics used in aircraft.

cargo
Goods or merchandise transported by ship, airplane, truck, or train.

civilian
A person not serving in the armed forces.

damage control
Aboard a ship, the measures taken to keep the ship safe and secure when dangerous situations occur (like fire, flooding, or accidents).

elite
Superior in some way.

enlist
To voluntarily join the military.

GED
A General Education Development certificate, which proves a person's high school–level education.

intelligence
Information that is of military or political value.

interdict
To forbid.

manual dexterity
The ability to use one's hands with coordination to grasp and manipulate things.

maritime
Related to the sea.

marksmanship
The skill of shooting at and hitting a target.

Mayday
An international signal used as a distress call for help.

rank
An individual's position in military hierarchy.

recruit
A person who has decided to enlist in the military.

waterways
Bodies of water, such as rivers, canals, and lakes, that can be traveled or navigated.

ADDITIONAL RESOURCES

Selected Bibliography

Clairmont, Nicholas. "Flying Rescue Missions in the Most Remote Reaches of the U.S.," *Atlantic*, 26 Oct. 2016. theatlantic.com. Accessed 2 Dec. 2019.

"Fires, Floods, and Fixes – How the Damage Controlman Keeps Us Safe," *Coast Guard Mid Atlantic*, 10 Apr. 2018. midatlantic.coastguard.dodlive.mil. Accessed 2 Dec. 2019.

Thiesen, William H. "The Long Blue Line: Coast Guard Responders During Record-Setting Hurricane Katrina," *Coast Guard Compass*, 25 Aug. 2016. compass.coastguard.blog. Accessed 2 Dec. 2019.

Further Readings

Allman, Toney. *Careers in the US Coast Guard*. ReferencePoint Press, 2016.

Mooney, Carla. *US Navy*. Abdo, 2021.

Radley, Gail. *US Marine Corps*. Abdo, 2021.

Online Resources

To learn more about the US Coast Guard, please visit **abdobooklinks.com** or scan this QR code. These links are routinely monitored and updated to provide the most current information available.

More Information

For more information on this subject, contact or visit the following organizations:

Coast Guard Foundation
394 Taugwonk Rd.
Stonington, CT 06378
860-535-0786
coastguardfoundation.org

This nonprofit organization provides lots of helpful information about the coast guard on its website. The foundation provides education, support, and relief to coast guard members and their families.

US Coast Guard Academy
31 Mohegan Ave.
New London, CT 06320
800-883-8724
uscga.edu

The US Coast Guard Academy is a competitive military college that offers bachelor of science degrees in engineering and other professional majors. Students are commissioned as ensigns in the coast guard when they graduate. The academy also has a museum that is open for visitors.

SOURCE NOTES

CHAPTER 1. FLYING INTO THE STORM

1. "US Coast Guard Facts." *US Coast Guard*, Jan. 2020, uscgboating.org. Accessed 8 Jan. 2020.
2. Nicholas Clairmont. "Flying Rescue Missions in the Most Remote Reaches of the US." *Atlantic*, 26 Oct. 2016, theatlantic.com. Accessed 8 Jan. 2020.
3. Clairmont, "Flying Rescue Missions."
4. Clairmont, "Flying Rescue Missions."
5. "Active-Duty Enlisted FAQ." *GoCoastGuard*, 2019, gocoastguard.com. Accessed 8 Jan. 2020.
6. "We Are the US Coast Guard." *GoCoastGuard*, 2019, gocoastguard.com. Accessed 8 Jan. 2020.

CHAPTER 2. THE HISTORY OF THE US COAST GUARD

1. "Timeline 1700s–1800s." *United States Coast Guard*, n.d., history.uscg.mil. Accessed 5 Sept. 2019.
2. "Cutters." *United States Coast Guard*, n.d., dco.uscg.mil. Accessed 8 Jan. 2020.
3. "Timeline 1700s–1800s."
4. Diana Honings. "Coast Guard Heroes: Keeper Ida Lewis." *Coast Guard Compass*, 18 Oct. 2015, compass.coastguard.blog. Accessed 8 Jan. 2020.
5. Malcolm F. Willoughby. *Rum War at Sea*. United States Government Printing Office, 1964. 163.
6. "War on Drugs." *History,* 17 Dec. 2019, history.com. Accessed 8 Jan. 2020.
7. "Alcoast 253/19–Aug 2019 Coast Guard's 229th Birthday." *United States Coast Guard*, Aug. 2019, content.godelivery.com. Accessed 8 Jan. 2020.
8. "Alcoast 253/19–Aug 2019 Coast Guard's 229th Birthday."
9. "Alcoast 253/19–Aug 2019 Coast Guard's 229th Birthday."

CHAPTER 3. THE US COAST GUARD TODAY

1. "The Coast Guard: America's Oldest Maritime Defenders." *Go Coast Guard*, 2019, gocoastguard.com. Accessed 8 Jan. 2020.
2. "The Coast Guard: America's Oldest Maritime Defenders."
3. "About the USCGA." *United States Coast Guard Academy*, 2020, uscga.edu. Accessed 8 Jan. 2020.
4. "Workforce." *United States Coast Guard*, n.d., work.uscg.mil. Accessed 19 Sept. 2019.
5. "Monthly Rates of Basic Pay (Commissioned Officer) - Effective January 1, 2020." *Defense Finance and Accounting Service*, 27 Dec. 2019, dfas.mil. Accessed 8 Jan. 2020.
6. "Workforce."
7. "A Ride with the Coast Guard Reserve." *YouTube,* uploaded by Today's Military, 9 Oct. 2012. youtube.com. Accessed 8 Jan. 2020.
8. Taylor Sienkiewicz. "ASVAB Test Prep: How to Get the Score You Want on the ASVAB." *Peterson's*, 15 Nov. 2018, petersons.com. Accessed 8 Jan. 2020.
9. "About the Auxiliary." *United States Coast Guard Auxiliary*, n.d., cgaux.org. Accessed 8 Jan. 2020.
10. "Workforce."

11. William H. Thiesen. "The Long Blue Line: Coast Guard Responders During Record-Setting Hurricane Katrina." *Coast Guard Compass*, 25 Aug. 2016, compass.coastguard.blog. Accessed 8 Jan. 2020.

CHAPTER 4. BOATSWAIN'S MATE

1. Dan Bender. "Boat Forces Tour—Boatswain's Mate 'A' School." *Coast Guard Compass*, 6 Oct. 2010, compass.coastguard.blog. Accessed 8 Jan. 2020.
2. "US Coast Guard Jobs: Boatswain's Mate (BM)." *Facebook*, uploaded by GoCoastGuard, 1 Dec. 2016. facebook.com. Accessed 8 Jan. 2020.
3. "The Cutters, Boats, and Aircraft of the US Coast Guard." *United States Coast Guard*, n.d., uscg.mil. Accessed 8 Jan. 2020.
4. NyxoLyno Cangemi. "Vermont Native Takes On the Arctic Ice." *Coast Guard Compass*, 22 Oct. 2018, compass.coastguard.blog. Accessed 8 Jan. 2020.
5. "US Coast Guard Jobs: Boatswain's Mate (BM)."
6. "Philip Kiley." *Today's Military*, 2020, todaysmilitary.com. Accessed 8 Jan. 2020.

CHAPTER 5. MARITIME ENFORCEMENT SPECIALIST

1. "The Coast Guard: America's Oldest Maritime Defenders." *Go Coast Guard*, 2019, gocoastguard.com. Accessed 8 Jan. 2020.
2. Melissa Leake. "Honor, Respect, Devotion to Duty: ME1 Jesse Pitrelli, ME1 Peter Purcell." *Coast Guard Compass*, 11 Mar. 2016, compass.coastguard.blog. Accessed 8 Jan. 2020.
3. "USCG Appoints First Woman Warrant Officer in Maritime Enforcement." *Safety4Sea*, 19 June 2019, safety4sea.com. Accessed 8 Jan. 2020.
4. "Coast Guard Jobs: Maritime Enforcement Specialist (ME)." *YouTube*, uploaded by GoCoastGuard, 16 June 2016, youtube.com. Accessed 8 Jan. 2020.
5. Joshua Canup. "What the Day Demands." *Coast Guard Mid Atlantic*, 2 Oct. 2015, midatlantic.coastguard.dodlive.mil. Accessed 8 Jan. 2020.

CHAPTER 6. DAMAGE CONTROLMAN

1. "View Coast Guard Job Descriptions." *Go Coast Guard*, 2019, gocoastguard.com. Accessed 8 Jan. 2020.
2. "Fires, Floods and Fixes – How the Damage Controlman Keeps Us Safe." *Coast Guard Mid Atlantic*, 10 Apr. 2018, midatlantic.coastguard.dodlive.mil. Accessed 8 Jan. 2020.
3. "Timothy Florez Adams." *Today's Military*, 2020, todaysmilitary.com. Accessed 8 Jan. 2020.
4. Michael De Nyse. "Damage Control, Not Damage Repair – Keeping an Aging Cutter Active." *Coast Guard Compass*, 26 June 2018, compass.coastguard.blog. Accessed 8 Jan. 2020.
5. "Fires, Floods and Fixes – How the Damage Controlman Keeps Us Safe."
6. "Fires, Floods and Fixes – How the Damage Controlman Keeps Us Safe."
7. De Nyse, "Damage Control, Not Damage Repair."
8. "Timothy Florez Adams."

SOURCE NOTES CONTINUED

9. "Fires, Floods and Fixes – How the Damage Controlman Keeps Us Safe."
10. "America's Tall Ship." *United States Coast Guard Academy*, 2020, uscga.edu. Accessed 8 Jan. 2020.

CHAPTER 7. AVIATOR

1. Nicholas Clairmont. "Flying Rescue Missions in the Most Remote Reaches of the US." *Atlantic*, 26 Oct. 2016, theatlantic.com. Accessed 8 Jan. 2020.
2. "Direct Commission Aviator (DCA)." *Go Coast Guard*, 2019, gocoastguard.com. Accessed 8 Jan. 2020.
3. "The Cutters, Boats, and Aircraft of the US Coast Guard." *United States Coast Guard*, n.d., uscg.mil. Accessed 8 Jan. 2020.
4. "Flight School." *United States Coast Guard Academy*, 2019, uscga.edu. Accessed 8 Jan. 2020.
5. Ethan Genter. "Astronauts Discuss How the Coast Guard Prepared Them for NASA." *Military*, 21 May 2018, military.com. Accessed 8 Jan. 2020.
6. David Lau. "Women of the Coast Guard Aviation Maintenance Technician Specialty." *Aviation Maintenance*, 22 Aug. 2018, avm-mag.com. Accessed 8 Jan. 2020.
7. Shannon H. Polson. "Coast Guard Pilot Chooses the Mission, and Finds Another." *Medium*, 17 Apr. 2018, medium.com. Accessed 8 Jan. 2020.
8. Lau, "Women of the Coast Guard."
9. Lau, "Women of the Coast Guard."

CHAPTER 8. PHARMACIST

1. Kate Traynor. "Readiness, Variety Are Hallmarks of Coast Guard Pharmacy." *ASHP*, 1 Feb. 2017, ashp.org. Accessed 8 Jan. 2020.
2. Traynor, "Readiness, Variety Are Hallmarks of Coast Guard Pharmacy."
3. Terri D'Arrigo. "Always Ready: United States Coast Guard Pharmacists Are Masters of Multitasking." *American Pharmacists Association*, 24 Apr. 2017, pharmacist.com. Accessed 8 Jan. 2020.
4. Lisa Novak. "Still Going Strong after 214 Years Together: The US Coast Guard and the US Public Health Service." *Coast Guard Compass*, 14 May 2012, compass.coastguard.blog. Accessed 8 Jan. 2020.
5. D'Arrigo, "Always Ready: United States Coast Guard Pharmacists Are Masters of Multitasking."
6. Traynor, "Readiness, Variety Are Hallmarks of Coast Guard Pharmacy."
7. Traynor, "Readiness, Variety Are Hallmarks of Coast Guard Pharmacy."

CHAPTER 9. AVIATION SURVIVAL TECHNICIAN

1. Julia Bergman. "Coast Guard Members Talk about Being a Rescue Swimmer." *The Day*, 24 Sept. 2018, theday.com. Accessed 8 Jan. 2020.
2. Shannon H. Polson. "This Woman Was the First to Complete Coast Guard Rescue Swimmer Training, and Serve." *Medium*, 11 Nov. 2017, medium.com. Accessed 8 Jan. 2020.
3. "A Day in the Life: Coast Guard Rescue Swimmer." *YouTube*, uploaded by CoastGuardNews, 9 Sept. 2014, youtube.com. Accessed 8 Jan. 2020.
4. Mario Vittone. "The World's Greatest Job: How Rescue Swimmers Are Made." *Soundings*, 19 Apr. 2018, soundingsonline.com. Accessed 15 Jan. 2020.

5. Vittone, "The World's Greatest Job: How Rescue Swimmers Are Made."
6. "Coast Guard Jobs: Rescue Swimmers, the Aviation Survival Technician (AST)." *YouTube*, uploaded by GoCoastGuard, 16 June 2016, youtube.com. Accessed 8 Jan. 2020.

CHAPTER 10. MARINE SCIENCE TECHNICIAN

1. Susan Biemesderfer. "Jeff Gregg / Cherokee and Blackfoot / US Coast Guard / Marine Science Technician (MST1)." *Winds of Change*, 1 Apr. 2017, woc.aises.org. Accessed 8 Jan. 2020.
2. Forrest PhiferSpens. "Why I Serve: MST1 Forrest PhiferSpens." *Coast Guard Compass*, 31 July 2013, compass.coastguard.blog. Accessed 8 Jan. 2020.
3. William Thiesen. "225 Years of Service to Nation: Marine Environmental Protection." *Coast Guard Compass*, 21 July 2015, compass.coastguard.blog. Accessed 8 Jan. 2020.
4. Biemesderfer, "Jeff Gregg."
5. "Coast Guard Jobs: Marine Science Technician (MST)." *YouTube*, uploaded by GoCoastGuard, 16 June 2019, youtube.com. Accessed 8 Jan. 2020.
6. "Coast Guard Jobs: Marine Science Technician (MST)."
7. "Ajia Brown." *United States Coast Guard Academy*, 2020, uscga.edu. Accessed 8 Jan. 2020.
8. "What to Expect." *United States Coast Guard Academy*, 2020, uscga.edu. Accessed 8 Jan. 2020.
9. NyxoLyno Cangemi. "Out of His Native Element: El Paso Native Trades Desert Sands for Arctic Waters." *Coast Guard Compass*, 24 Oct. 2018, compass.coastguard.blog. Accessed 8 Jan. 2020.

INDEX

Academy Introduction Mission (AIM), 96
Act to Create the Coast Guard, 16
active duty, 10, 29–30, 32, 49, 50, 69, 76
allowance, 29
apprentice, 11, 31
Armed Services Vocational Aptitude Battery (ASVAB), 9, 30, 32
aviation maintenance technician (AMT), 69, 71–72
aviation survival technician (AST), 83, 85, 87–88, 91
aviator, 64, 66–69, 71, 73

bachelor's degree, 27, 73, 81
Barringer, Amy, 50
basic training, 10, 30, 37, 41, 47
benefits, 30, 34
boatswain, 38–45, 98
boot camp, 37, 44
Bruckenthal, Nathan, 58
Bush, George W., 35

cadets, 27, 61, 67
Cape May, New Jersey, 30, 37
cargo, 19, 66, 69–70, 91
Coast Guard Academy, US, 27, 61, 67, 69, 96
Coast Guard Auxiliary, US, 33–34
Coast Guard Aviation Training Center, 68
Coast Guard Reserve, US, 30, 44, 69, 94
Coast Guard Training Center, 40
college, 10–11, 27, 29, 30, 34, 67, 71, 76, 79, 81, 96, 99
College Student Pre-Commissioning Initiative (CSPI), 34, 67
Congress, US, 12–13, 33, 84
coxswain, 40–41
cutters, 13–14, 16, 18–20, 38–39, 41–42, 45, 53, 57–60, 61, 63, 72, 73, 76

damage controlman (DC), 54–55, 57–58, 60–63,
Deepwater Horizon, 94
Department of Homeland Security, 9–10, 20, 25–26
Department of Transportation, 20
disasters, 25, 35, 54, 57, 66, 77, 95
drugs, 10, 19–20, 27, 48, 51, 64, 75, 81

endurance, 51, 86, 91
enlistment, 9–10, 16, 29–31, 38, 40, 43, 45, 47, 50, 53, 54, 66, 69, 71, 73, 76, 81, 99
environment, 24–28, 34, 41, 64, 71, 74, 79, 92, 94–96, 98–99

Faulkner, Sara, 85
firefighting, 11, 37, 57, 60, 62, 63, 77
first aid, 48, 53
fitness, 37, 50–51
flight training, 11, 67–68, 73
Fraser, Alexander, 15–16

gear, 90–91
GED, 45, 53, 91, 99
Great Lakes, 6, 28, 41

health services technician, 76, 79, 81
helicopters, 4–9, 35, 64–66, 69, 70–73, 84, 87, 88–91
homeland security missions, 26–27, 33, 66
housing, 29, 34
Hurricane Katrina, 35, 85

icebreaker ships, 6, 20, 29, 41
immigration, 48
inspections, 6, 17, 49, 76, 93, 97–99

110

law enforcement, 14, 26–27, 32, 34, 41–42, 44–45, 46–48, 51–53, 66, 71, 98
leadership, 34, 41–42, 44–45, 47, 53, 61, 96
Lewis, Ida, 15
lighthouses, 12–13, 15, 17, 28

marine science technician, 92–99
maritime enforcement specialist, 46–53, 98
math, 32, 63, 73, 95, 99
medicine, 76–77, 80–81
migrants, 27

National Aeronautics and Space Administration (NASA), 67
navigation, 5, 17, 19, 27–28, 38–40, 43–45, 61, 70, 77, 87
New London, Connecticut, 11, 27, 68, 99
non–homeland security missions, 26–28

Officer Candidate School, 10–11, 34, 61
oil spill, 6, 94, 95–99

patrol, 13, 33, 42–43, 45, 66, 99
pharmacist, 74–81
pilot, 4–7, 9, 41, 45, 64–69, 71–73, 83–84, 90
plumbing, 55, 57, 60–63
pollution, 10, 33, 92–97, 99
Presidential Unit Citation, 35
Prohibition, 17–18

racial integration, 16
ratings, 10–11, 38–40, 47, 50, 61, 63, 98–99
regulations, 6, 26, 28, 93, 97
rescue swimmers, 6–7, 82–91
research, 27, 41
resources, 28, 48, 77, 94–95
Revenue Cutter Service, 14, 16
rum runners, 18

salary, 29–30, 34
seamanship, 37, 38–40, 43–44, 61
search and rescue, 7–9, 14, 27–28, 32–33, 35, 40–44, 64, 66, 71, 88
segregation, 16
September 11, 2001, 7, 20
smuggling, 14, 18–20, 27, 48, 51
special operations, 84–85
surfman, 40

technology, 20, 35, 40, 44, 61, 95
terrorism, 7, 20, 22, 26–27, 42, 47–49, 51, 65, 98
Treasury, US, 13–14, 20

US Public Health Service (USPHS) Commissioned Corps, 79–80

War on Drugs, 19
warrant officer, 31, 50
weather, 5, 7–8, 40, 82, 87, 90
welding, 55, 57, 60–63
Wilks' Flight Initiative (WiFI), 67
Wilson, Woodrow, 16
World Trade Center, 7
World War II, 18, 33

Yorktown, Virginia, 40–41, 60, 96

111

ABOUT THE AUTHOR

Donna B. McKinney

Donna B. McKinney is the author of more than ten nonfiction books for kids on topics ranging from science and technology to history to sports. Before she wrote for children, she spent many years writing about science and technology topics, such as chemistry, space science, and robotics, at the US Naval Research Laboratory in Washington, DC. She has a bachelor's degree in English from Campbell University and a master's in professional writing and editing from George Mason University. She lives in North Carolina.